_ .ibs!_ Cade yelle
a viper-gun glinti
pillion.

But even before h
hand flickered, and suddenly she ...
viper from the car window. As the bike swerved to
avoid the shot, Cade dragged the car into a screeching turn and sent it hurtling back towards the exit
ramp.

Raishe braced herself as they flashed back up the
ramp and out on to the street. But there Cade spun
the car into another howling, skidding turn, all the
way around, and then gave it full power – back the
way they had come. And Raishe had only begun to
look startled when they blasted back down onto the
ramp, and met the pursuing alley-bike head on.

The Occian driver was quick enough to start evasive
action, so the car hit the bike only a glancing blow.
Even so, the bike was flung aside, bouncing off the
wall and crashing down the ramp. As it came to a
sliding, spinning, grinding halt, Cade hit his brakes
to halt the car and Raishe leaped out with gun
ready . . .

Galaxy's Edge is the first title in an action-packed
trilogy set on far-off worlds.

DOUGLAS HILL

CADE

①

GALAXY'S EDGE

BANTAM BOOKS

TORONTO • NEW YORK • LONDON • SYDNEY • AUCKLAND

CADE: GALAXY'S EDGE
A BANTAM BOOK: 0 553 503340

First publication in Great Britain

PRINTING HISTORY
Bantam edition published 1996

Set in 11/14pt Linotype Palatino by
Phoenix Typesetting, Ilkley, West Yorkshire.

Bantam Books are published by Transworld Publishers Ltd,
61–63 Uxbridge Road, Ealing, London W5 5SA,
in Australia by Transworld Publishers (Australia) Pty. Ltd,
15–25 Helles Avenue, Moorebank, NSW 2170,
and in New Zealand by Transworld Publishers (NZ) Ltd,
3 William Pickering Drive, Albany, Auckland.

Made and printed in Great Britain by
Cox & Wyman Ltd, Reading, Berks.

for MICHAEL and ROSEMARY
and all these new beginnings

1

Escape from Breell

If this is an open prison, Cade thought, lead me to a closed one. Like one of those olden-day dungeons – cool and damp and peaceful . . .

He prodded glumly with his fend-spear at the powdery blue dust ahead of him, watching it swirl and settle, aware that he had thought the same thing every day since he had been sentenced. And that there were all too many days ahead when he would be thinking it again. Lifting his gaze, he stared out over the blue desert that stretched to the horizon, its barren emptiness offering a perfect image of the confinement that also stretched before him.

The desert covered most of a large island on a planet named Breell. Decades before, after humans had colonized Breell, they had built a prison – an open prison – on one corner of the island. Inevitably, a time had come when it needed expanding. But it could only be expanded outwards, on to the desert, which meant that the blue barrenness had to be tamed and reclaimed.

To begin that work, a labour force had been created from the convict population already on the island.

The convicts knew very well why they had been chosen. The desert was highly dangerous – and they were wholly expendable.

Cade had heard plenty of stories about people who had tried to escape from the prison, over the years, by trying to cross the desert. Those who had survived thirst and heat-stroke, and the hostile life-forms that lived their alien lives on or under the blue sand, had in the end been halted at the island's edge by the barrier of Breell's burningly acid sea.

A very open prison, Cade thought. Because there are so many ways open to you to get killed . . .

'Pay *heed*, pinch-face!'

The harsh throaty growl came from one side, making him jump. But he made no reply, since he was used to both the heavily accented voice and the hostility behind it. He merely glanced warily at the tall inhuman being who was also probing with a fend-spear at the blue dust, while glaring at Cade for letting his attention wander.

The alien, properly called an Occian, was more or less humanoid, lean and stringy with a broad head, wide mouth and bulging eyes. His greyish skin was thick, ridged and blotchy, and there was a slight webbing between the bony fingers.

The Occians were amphibious, and so had been nicknamed 'Phibs' – a numerous, aggressive species who from the beginning of star-travel had clashed with the numerous and aggressive *human* expansion. More decades earlier, that clash had sparked a short but costly war between humans and Occians, after which the Human Commonwealth and the Occian Unity had begun a continuing period of total separation, wary competition and intense mutual dislike.

The dislike operated as intensely among individuals as well, perhaps especially in a prison. Cade certainly had no great liking for Phibs, nor – usually – much interest in them. And yet, ever since the desert work had begun, Cade had made every effort to be teamed up as often as possible with that particular Occian prisoner for each day's work.

He had done so because he knew that, somewhere on its reptilian person, that particular Occian carried a mysterious object that the alien believed to be hugely valuable, perhaps priceless.

Cade knew all that because each night, when the labour force had been taken back to their quarters in the main, original prison, that Occian – surrounded by the two or three other Phib prisoners, keeping apart from humans as always – brought out the object and gloated over it. With Cade eavesdropping intently, while never showing the smallest sign that, unusually for a human, he had some grasp of the Occian language.

Ever since he had first overheard one of those gloating sessions, the unknown object had dominated Cade's yearnings and daydreams – along with an assortment of fantasies about escape. But then, such dreams had always been what had kept Cade going – and getting into trouble . . .

He was a young man, nearly twenty human years old – not tall but well-built, solid and springy, trimmed down to leanness by poor food and desert labour. Prison rules required his curly brown hair to be shorter than he liked, just as they required him and the others in the working group to wear shapeless reflecting robes as protection against the fierce desert sun. Within the robe's hood Cade's face was boyishly good-looking, almost cherubic, with clear blue eyes and a ready smile that could be cheeky or cheerful or charming as the need arose.

His charm, and his appearance generally, had served him well on many worlds, in many different and seldom legal enterprises. Along with some other useful skills, it had helped him to live reasonably well much of the time, and otherwise to stay clear of various forms of law enforcement that became aware of him. Even after he had slipped up and been caught, on Breell, he had been able to win over some of the guards, and so to wheedle a number of favours – including that regular pairing with the Occian who owned the secret and valuable thing.

But no amount of human charm could hope to overcome the deep-rooted suspicion and aggressive hostility of an Occian. So all Cade could do, every day, was look longingly at the loose wrinkly skin of the Occian's throat – where an internal storage sac contained the valuable thing – and dream his unlikely dreams.

'*Move*, weak-skin!' the Occian snarled.

Cade jumped slightly again, realizing that he had stopped in his tracks and was staring all too obviously at the alien's throat. But the Phib had not seemed to notice – shuffling forward, muttering and growling as he probed the dust with the fend-spear. His mutterings, in Occian, expressed remarkably obscene views of Cade's ancestry, but as usual Cade's face betrayed not the tiniest hint that he understood. He merely pushed forward as well, wielding his own spear.

About thirty other robed and hooded convicts were spread out over the desert in a broad wavery arc, doing the same thing, stolidly watched by half-a-dozen guards. All the workers were nearly knee-deep in the blue dust, their legs armoured with thigh-high ceramalloy boots against burrowing creatures lurking beneath the desert surface. The fend-spears that they carried,

11

useless as weapons, resembled long oversized forks whose prongs emitted mild electroblasts that distressed the desert life-forms enough to force them to the surface. Then the guards would stun them with real weapons – electroguns called *rattlers*, firing a focused blast that could temporarily knock out most nervous systems. And the stunned life-forms would be taken away to be humanely dealt with elsewhere.

At least, that was the theory. But the protective boots did not always protect, and the guards were not always alert or quick enough. Cade had already seen two prisoners badly hurt by big, furious dust-eels that spat pellets of their own poisonous dung, and had himself once been barely quick enough to avoid a whipping, venomous tendril from a mobile spine-vine. And, he thought darkly as he shuffled forward next to the Occian, the odds are getting worse with every step I take.

Even as that thought formed, it seemed for an instant that his luck had finally run out – for a terrible eerie howling suddenly filled the desert air all around him. But he recognized the howl almost at once, and reacted to it in the same way as all the other convict workers. Tucking the handle of his fend-spear under his arm, he drew his hood tightly around his face and clamped his hands over his ears.

Even then the howling grew nearly painful as

a stubby-winged aircraft settled down towards the ground in a raging, choking tornado of blue dust. It landed slightly ahead of the prisoners and to one side, so that Cade and the Occian were nearest to it. And Cade peered through the dust at it with some curiosity, since it was one of the shuttles that carried the labour force back and forth from the main prison to the desert. It's too early, he thought, frowning. Where are they taking us now?

But then, as the dust settled, he saw that the shuttle was not taking but *bringing*. When the hatch opened, three convicts in robes and alloy boots clambered out, followed by a watchful guard with a rattler – and then by the shuttle pilot, who peered around with interest, showing that he had never made the desert run before. Enjoying the break in routine, Cade watched as the new prisoners were herded over to the other guards who had gathered to receive them. All the prisoners in the labour force had also stopped work to watch, their fend-spears idle. Even the particular Occian who was paired with Cade was watching, growling faintly as if annoyed by the human activity.

In that still moment, without warning, the Occian's growl expanded into a shrill and shocking scream of agony – when from the sand at his feet the writhing tangle of a big spine-vine burst out and flung a tendril like a thorny whip around the Occian's unprotected wrist.

And the scream was still in its first micro-second when Cade saw, in his mind's eye, unexpected but perfectly clear, a step-by-step plan of exactly what he was going to do.

The alien began to fall, his scream cut off as the vine's poison stunned and paralysed him. And the unconscious alien body had barely hit the ground when Cade jabbed at the vine with his spear to drive it back, then reached down, pried open the Occian's mouth and thrust his hand into the slightly slimy throat. There, in the bulge of the storage sac, his fumbling fingers closed on a small flat ovoid that felt like plastic, and he jerked it out with a triumphant grin.

Tucking the ovoid into a boot-top, he sprang to his feet. Only seconds had passed since the Occian's scream, and everyone else was only beginning to react – the guards starting to rush forward, the Occian prisoners starting to howl in outrage as they saw the theft. By then, also, the spine-vine had begun to burrow back into the sand. But Cade was still moving at full speed, still seeing his plan of action laid out in his mind as if he had been working on it for a year.

Plunging his spear into the sand under the vine, he scooped it up, straining a little under its weight, dodging a trailing tendril – then used the spear's long handle like a lever to swing the vine up into the air, and throw it. It hurtled away in a curving arc, tendrils thrashing, aimed at the group of guards rushing towards Cade. Yelling in alarm, the guards scattered, stumbling in the powdery sand as they desperately tried to avoid the deadly thorns.

With that head start, Cade sprinted away. Towards the shuttle.

The pilot was still standing by the open hatch, gaping and bewildered. Unaware that the fend-spear was harmless, he shied back as Cade threatened him with its prongs. And then Cade tossed the spear aside and leaped into the ship, slapping a hand on to the switch that closed the hatch just as the first ill-aimed bursts from the guards' rattlers hissed around him.

Flinging himself into the pilot's seat at the shuttle controls, Cade grinned at the familiar, mostly pre-programmed guidance system. And he was laughing aloud as he took the shuttle up in another blue dust-storm, and powered away into the desert sky.

2

The Price of a World

The unoriginally named Black Hole Club stood on a shabby back street in the largest city on the planet Breell. The club offered a limited range of food, a variety of intoxicating drinks from many worlds and abundant mild narcotics. All that, plus a few third-rate entertainers at weekends, seldom brought in more than a handful of customers at any time.

So the club had acquired only four silent, huddled patrons on the rain-dampened afternoon when the robed and hooded stranger entered.

Of course, to the lone steward working in the club, most customers on any day were strangers. And many of them also kept themselves well covered – which to the steward always seemed highly comical, since he was one of the dwarfish, orange-skinned alien species from the planet Illiya. The humanoid Illiyans mostly wore nothing at all on their home world and colony worlds, while on other planets they yielded to more modest custom only with minimal kilts, like the shiny purple one worn by the steward.

Yet no sign of his amusement showed in the steward's huge dark eyes as the over-dressed stranger approached. Not even when the steward noticed the stranger's soiled and ill-fitting coveralls beneath the robe, and his clumping, sloppily over-large boots.

'Is Aphoz around?' the stranger asked, in the language of the Human Commonwealth, his voice sounding youthful though his face was hidden in the hood's shadows.

'I don't know the name,' the steward said with automatic caution.

The hooded human sighed. 'Tall skinny bald man, scarred cheek, broken nose, a finger missing on one hand. You couldn't miss him. Especially when he *owns* this place.'

'I don't know what you mean,' the Illiyan said blankly.

The hooded one sighed again. 'Just tell him I want to see him. You can't really think I'm a Civil Patrolman modelling a glamorous new-style uniform.'

The steward nearly smiled before catching himself. 'Maybe you could give me your name?'

'That's really funny,' the hooded one said flatly. 'Just get Aphoz. He knows my name.'

The steward remained still. 'So you say. But you could be anyone.'

'In fact,' the hooded one said, sounding like he was speaking through clenched teeth, 'I'm *someone*. And if you don't go and get Aphoz . . .'

He stopped – because the steward had touched a small stud on his belt, and a mirror on a side wall had opened like a door. In the doorway stood a bulky and remarkably ugly human holding a short and equally ugly bar of dark metal that had somehow been tied in a crude knot, perhaps by its wielder's huge hands.

As he stepped out, the other four customers rose in a flurry and bolted out of the front door. But the hooded figure paid no attention. He simply opened his robe at the front, to show the heavy shape of a hand-gun tucked into his waistband. The unmistakeable shape of a pyro-gun, which fired focused bursts of pure incinerating flame.

Seeing it, the club-wielder and the steward both went very still. And in that frozen moment, through the doorway that the mirror had covered, a tall bony man emerged who exactly fitted the description given by the hooded one.

'Aphoz!' said the hooded one with some relief. 'Don't you recognize voices any more?'

'I was busy,' said the tall man, Aphoz, scowling. 'An' now you've scared off my customers, I hope you're at least gonna buy a drink.'

'Not exactly,' said the hooded one, moving

towards the doorway. 'But you'll buy me one when I tell you what I've got for you.'

Shaking his head, the tall man led the way back to a small room like an office, with a cheap Netlink terminal and other info-tech items scattered on rickety shelves and a cluttered table. There the tall man kicked the door shut and wheeled on his visitor.

'Lord's sake, Jaxie!' he snarled. 'What're you doin', comin' here?'

'Call me *Cade*,' said Cade, throwing back his hood and glaring. 'And you could be a *little* pleased to see me.'

Aphoz snorted. 'Could I? Look at you! You *tryin'* to get picked up? An' me along with you?'

Cade shrugged. 'I didn't exactly have time to pack my bags when I left. But I know I wasn't spotted, coming here.'

'Not yet, maybe,' Aphoz growled. 'But the Civs know we're pals, an' they were sniffin' round here the day after you broke out, an' most every day since.'

Cade looked unconcerned. 'Let them sniff. Did they tell you anything about me?'

'Some,' Aphoz nodded, settling onto a stained sofa. 'Said you stole a shuttle an' took off from that island jail about nine, ten days ago. An' first, if they got it right, you robbed a Phib who got hurt.' He lounged back, seeming at ease and unconcerned – but his close-set eyes had begun to glitter hungrily. 'What'd you steal, Ja . . . Cade?'

Cade smiled knowingly. 'Never mind. That's not what I've got for you. I want to sell you the shuttle, so I can get some things I need and get off Breell.'

'What if I don't wanna buy?' Aphoz asked sourly. 'You gonna pull that pyro an' *make* me do it? Get back at me 'cause you got jailed?'

Cade's smile became warm and cajoling. 'If I wanted to do that, do you think I'd be here offering you a sweet deal? You know me better than that. We were *partners*, Aph – and that hasn't changed just because things went wrong and I got nabbed.' He laughed. 'For all we know, there might've really *been* spallerium on that asteroid we were selling.'

Aphoz echoed his laughter. 'It was a good game, while it lasted,' he said. 'I always said you could sell sand to a dust-eel when you get goin'. Just like you're tryin' to sell me a shuttle, now.' Grinning, he studied Cade thoughtfully, then slowly nodded. 'An' I guess I'm gonna buy,' he went on. 'You got it hid somewhere safe?'

'That's what I've been doing since I got away,' Cade replied. 'Getting it near the city without being seen – tucking it away where no one will spot it – then getting myself here just as carefully.'

Aphoz looked grave. 'You'll have to stay careful, too, pal. Soon it won't just be Civs lookin' for you. If you took somethin' important from that Phib in jail, you could have lizard-faces comin' at you from all directions when the news gets out. You know Phibs. They don't forget or forgive, specially when it's a human done 'em wrong.'

Cade's cajoling smile reappeared. 'All the more reason for me to get moving. Come on, Aph. I'll take any reasonable price – then I'll be out of here, and your worries will be over.'

Again Aphoz thought for a moment, then carefully named a sum in human-world currency.

Cade grimaced. 'You're not feeling generous, are you? But I'm in no position to haggle. I'll take it.'

'I wouldn't cheat you, pal,' Aphoz said virtuously. 'I'm buyin' the thing sight unseen, remember. Where *is* it, anyway?'

'No offence, Aph,' Cade replied, 'but I'll tell you that when I have cash in hand.'

The other man frowned. 'That's not very trustin' . . . An' you want cash?' He heaved himself to his feet. 'I s'pose it makes sense. Hang on while I go get it together.'

Cade raised a restraining hand. 'Aph – I'd be really upset if anything was said about me to your steward, or anyone else.'

Aphoz looked injured. 'You don't hafta be like

that. I wouldn't say a word.' He offered a reassuring smile. 'In fact, I'll bring us a bottle an' some eats, along with the cash. An' I'll throw in some clothes for you as well, that fit a bit better.'

Cade glanced down at himself. 'Some of this stuff was on the shuttle, so I grabbed it.' Then he looked at Aphoz again, his eyes steady. 'And the pyro was on the shuttle too, Aph. Let's not forget that.'

'No chance,' Aphoz said quickly. 'You just relax now, an' I'll get things organized.'

'One more thing,' Cade said. 'Does this junk terminal of yours have a reader function?'

As before, Aphoz's eyes became hungrily curious, but his voice and his nod both seemed indifferent. 'Sure – help yourself. I won't be long.'

When he had left, Cade went to inspect the door and its frame, then made a quick but thorough examination of the room's walls. Finally, with a wry smile, he moved to the terminal, taking from his pocket the small plastic ovoid that had once lodged in a Phib's storage sac. And his hands were shaking slightly as he pried the ovoid open and brought out a short, paper-thin strip of slightly flexible material, which gleamed as if it was glass or polished metal.

In fact it was a special form of silicon, called a *slice*, which was a common way to store and transport a small portion of data. Cade had gazed at it many times since his escape from the desert, but until then he had had no access to a reader that would reveal its secret.

A secret that – as the Phib who had owned it had once said, during one of his sessions of gloating – was worth 'the price of a world'.

Switching on the terminal, Cade inserted the slice. At once his brow furrowed as a stream of meaningless and jumbled symbols began to scroll across the screen. It's in code, he thought – or some Phib mystery.

But then his gaze sharpened. The parade of jumbled symbols slowed and halted, and was then followed by two lines of letters and numerals that seemed to be the last data on the slice. And Cade did know what *those* two lines meant. A great many people in the galaxy would have recognized them – if, like Cade, they were given to improbable dreams and yearnings.

For some moments he sat quite still, staring wide-eyed at the screen while questions and doubts and hopes and a pure wild excitement swarmed through his mind. But then a sound beyond the door alerted him. Swiftly he drew the slice from the terminal, put it back in its case and the case in his pocket, switched off the screen, and was lounging casually in a chair when Aphoz struggled back into the room, somewhat burdened.

The burden included a tray with a bottle, two

glasses and a plate of greasy-looking snacks, while under one arm Aphoz was awkwardly clutching a bundle of clothing. But Cade was more interested in a different bundle – a huge sheaf of thin plastic rectangles, magni-printed in shades of green, that were the legal currency of the Human Commonwealth.

'You're getting a shuttle very cheaply,' Cade remarked after he had counted the cash.

Aphoz grinned and shrugged. 'An' you're gettin' off Breell, so we're both happy.'

Cade nodded, accepted the glass of golden liquid that Aphoz poured for him and prodded at the bundle of clothing. 'This looks fine, Aph,' he said. 'I'm obliged.'

He set the glass down untasted, and with some relief began to change into the clothes Aphoz had brought – a simple tunic, trousers and shoes, unremarkable in colour or style, all fitting reasonably well. As he did so he still looked entirely relaxed and casual – but he did not fail to notice the predatory glint in Aphoz's eyes while watching Cade transfer the bundle of cash and the small plastic case to his new pockets. Nor did he miss the fact that Aphoz had also not touched his drink. And so, despite his relaxed manner, the pyro-gun was never far from Cade's hand at every moment.

Then Aphoz lifted his glass. 'Drink up, pal.

This is special. You won't have had anythin' like this where you been this past while.'

Cade nodded slightly, but did not reach for his drink. Instead, he took the pyro-gun in his hand, not pointing it at anything but hefting it thoughtfully. 'I'm sure it's special,' he said evenly. 'You've probably got a lot of special stuff here. All designed to help you do deals and make money and stay out of harm's way.'

Aphoz's eyes narrowed. 'What's that s'posed to mean?'

Cade smiled. 'While you were gone just now, Aph, I had a look around. And I also had a little bet with myself. I bet that while you were getting my cash and all, you'd be doing another deal – probably with the Civs. Maybe adding something to the booze, too.'

He lifted the gun, aiming it at the centre of Aphoz's face, silencing the other man's reply and bringing a sheen of sweat on his bony face. In that moment, they both heard sudden noises from out in the main area of the club – the stamp of feet, the muffled sound of voices.

'What do you know,' Cade said grimly. 'I think I won my bet.'

He moved past Aphoz, keeping the gun steady, and touched a small stud on the door-frame that he had spotted earlier. At once a strange shimmer appeared over the doorway – a privacy barrier, which would resist most attempts to force the door.

'I'd also bet,' he went on calmly, 'that you have another way out of here – a private escape hatch. Right?' He lowered the gun's muzzle to point at Aphoz's groin. 'So open it up, Aph. Or you can spend the Civs' money on treatment for burns in a very painful place.'

Aphoz was sweating heavily, staring at the unwavering gun. 'Take it easy, Jax . . . Cade,' he stammered. 'It's here.'

He picked up a pocket-sized transmitter from the clutter on the table and touched a button. At the other end of the room, a patch of bare wall at once developed a clean straight crack, which widened and opened like the iris of an eye. Beyond it stretched a darkened empty hallway, belonging to the building next door.

Still smiling, Cade plucked the transmitter from Aphoz's hand, then backed towards the iris-opening while, beyond the other door, a burst of shouts and clatterings arose as the privacy barrier was discovered.

'I'll take the transmitter, so this back door doesn't open up again too soon,' he said cheerily, stepping out through the iris-opening. Then he paused on that threshold, holding up the pyro-gun. 'And since this gun comes from the shuttle that you've just bought, you'd better have it too.' His grin widened. 'I'm sorry to say that I couldn't find any charges for it. It's empty.'

He threw the gun back into the room with Aphoz, then touched the transmitter button. The iris-opening instantly closed, as if the wall was shutting an eye in a knowing wink. Then he dropped the transmitter and trotted away along the empty hall – aware of the pleasing bulk of the cash in one pocket, but even more aware of the small plastic case in another, and the mysterious, perhaps priceless data-slice that it held.

Codes can be broken, he was thinking as he made his escape. Especially when they contain data that a Phib called 'worth the price of a world'.

And, he thought, I know just *which* world he meant.

3

Tallyra

The immense Starliner had been powering along at maximum speed for several days after leaving the Xardoci system, the second-last stop on its route. Those days were taking the mighty ship along the last and longest leg of its transgalactic journey – towards a solar system that was unusually isolated, far from any constellation, cluster or nebula. In fact, on the charts that mapped the galactic spacelines, that system – a sun and three planets – was shown to be *farther* than any other from the busy, crowded centre of the civilized galaxy.

For that reason, the isolated system was often simply and graphically called 'the Edge'. And its one inhabited planet – an oxygen world, human-colonized, named Tallyra – was also known as the Edge-world.

It was of course not a true edge, or rim, or fringe. It was not at all like a jut of bare rock on a shoreline with nothing but sea beyond. But anyone who knew about it tended to imagine it rather like that, as an actual border-line, a distant and exciting frontier, a focus for various imaginings and yearnings. So, despite the cost, a great many people travelled to Tallyra to see if those imaginings were true, to try to fulfil those yearnings – or just for the thrill of being on the galaxy's Edge.

The Starliner had been mostly full for the first week or so, and it was still nearly half-full on that long final leg of its journey to Tallyra. But the reduced numbers gave the Chief Cabin Attendant some time to indulge in her favourite pastime – passenger-watching.

Alien passengers, of course, were the most fun to watch, but sadly for the Chief there were few of them on that Starliner. Just one Occian, who kept to himself as Occians usually did in human company. And no more than a handful from among the galaxy's only other intelligent beings.

Those other aliens came in three quite different species, each far less numerous than either humans or Occians. So they had banded together, for mutual benefit, in a loose federal arrangement called the *Aggregation*. The Chief had always wished that sometime the least numerous race of the Aggregation, the huge and voiceless Ylidai, would take up star-travel. Otherwise, there was little hope of an ordinary person ever seeing one. But the Ylidai seldom moved at all, apparently, let alone rode spaceships. So a devoted alien-watcher like the Chief had to content herself with the two other species within the Aggregation.

The wriggly Fsefsety tended to travel in happy, noisy, extended-family groups that were always good for a laugh. And there was one such group on that Starliner, to brighten the Chief's spare moments. There were several Illiyans as well, though the Chief was of the opinion that those orange-skinned beings would be a lot nicer if they didn't keep forgetting to wear their kilts, and if they didn't always *grab* at humans of either gender in such cheerfully uninhibited ways . . .

Also, along with the aliens on that half-full Starliner, there was no shortage of watchable humans among the passengers. One man, for instance, had a skin colour suggesting that he might be part-Illiyan, though the Chief had not thought that was possible. Another man, who spent most of every day being beaten at cube-chess by one of the GameNet machines, had a tiny furry alien pet on one shoulder, which passed all its waking time grooming its master's hair. Then there was that woman with the short dark hair and pale green eyes, who moved like a dancer – and who was certainly thin enough and pretty enough, in the Chief's envious opinion, to be one. Except that she looked oddly *dangerous*, somehow . . .

And, the Chief thought, there's the mystery

man, a member of one of the many weird religious sects of the Human Commonwealth – the Brotherhood of the Utter Dark. The Brothers looked almost scary in their long black cloaks, with their faces painted black and the shiny black epi-lenses on their eyes. But at least the Brotherhood splashed a lot of money around, always travelling to Tallyra to worship the vastness of the Deeps beyond the galactic Edge.

I wonder, the Chief mused, what they think is out there. And if they are painted black all over. And I wonder what this Brother has been *doing*, staying in his cabin by himself, day after day, ever since we picked him up on Pilifar V . . .

She smiled happily, savouring the puzzle. Whatever he's doing, she thought, he'll have to come out soon. We'll be shifting to normal space any minute now, and *everyone* likes to watch the approach to Tallyra. I wonder if he'll kneel down to pray or something . . .

Many quite different questions might have arisen in the Chief's mind if she had known other things about the mystery Brother. That, for instance, he had boarded the Starliner on Pilifar V after having earlier taken a short-hop flight from the planet Breell in a neighbouring system. That on the short-hop he had not been a Brother, but a grey-haired woman in a purple gown. That he had paid cash for his passage on both journeys, just as he had paid for the two disguises and other purchases on Breell.

And the Chief would have been wholly fascinated to have seen him at that moment, in front of a mirror in his tiny cabin, wearing only undershorts, with no part of his compact body painted black except his face. A boyishly good-looking, almost cherubic face beneath the make-up, with clear blue eyes and short curly brown hair . . .

Cade squeezed the small bulb of black colouring, dabbing another touch of it onto his forehead. Just a little while longer, he told himself. Then I can wash this stuff off, and dump that itchy cloak, and start being *me* again.

'I've *made* it,' he whispered aloud to his mirror image. 'I've got away, free and clear – with the price of a world in my pocket . . .'

He shivered suddenly, with excitement or tension or some unnameable dread. Then his whole body clenched with alarm as a firm knock shook the cabin's thin door.

'Sir?' said a woman's voice. 'Ah – Brother?'

'What is it?' Cade replied, putting a soulful tone into his voice.

'Chief Cabin Attendant here,' the Chief said through the door. 'I hope I'm not disturbing your . . . devotions, but I thought you'd like to know that we're about to come out of spin-drive into normal space. You could watch our approach to

Tallyra on the big screen in the lounge if you wish.'

'Thank you, Sister,' Cade intoned. 'You're very kind.'

Knowing that it would look odd if he failed to go, he pulled on the black cap that hid his hair, fitted the black lenses that shadowed his eyes and drew on the long black cloak that covered the rest of him. Just a little while more, he said to himself again, opening the door to see the hefty, middle-aged Chief waiting in the passage, curiosity bright in her eyes. But he brushed past her with a nod and set off at a stately pace towards the central passenger lounge.

As he went, he felt the eerie inner vibration that told him the Starliner had shut down its spin-field drive, which had taken it beyond true space-time and across half a galaxy in less than three human-world weeks. Now the passengers faced only a patience-testing half-hour while the ship drifted towards the huge docking station in orbit around Tallyra.

A glittering asteroid cluster was brightening the main screen as Cade entered the lounge. The other passengers, already gathered, glanced around at him automatically, but none of them showed more than a brief, vague interest. Still, he watched them carefully – especially noting the slender woman with short dark hair and luminous pale eyes, willowy and graceful in her sleeveless tunic and fitted leggings. I might have been glad of some interest from *her*, he thought, another time . . .

But then they all turned to the screen, murmuring with excitement at their first glimpse of the small bright disc that was Tallyra. And in that moment the voice of the Chief Cabin Attendant came over the intercom.

'Your attention, please. Passengers are reminded that, while Tallyra is a freeworld with almost no travel or import restrictions, all personal ID and other documentation should be kept available for presentation if required.'

She paused, as if for emphasis, then continued. 'Passengers are also advised to study the travel information, on cabin Netlinks, relating to Tallyran conditions and customs. Please especially note the details regarding personal safety and protection of valuables. Remember that Tallyra tends to display a lower level of law enforcement, moral concerns and . . . ah . . . *decorum* than you may be used to on your home worlds.'

Cade smiled to himself as he heard the comments among the passengers and the small cheer from the Illiyans. But that's what they're *here* for, he thought. To get away from laws and morals and *decorum* – to have a taste of freedom and a completely wild time, which has always been the speciality of the Edge . . .

By then the disc that was Tallyra was rapidly enlarging on the screen, and Cade saw that the planet's rotation had brought its four primary land masses into view – four enormous islands, lying at angles to one another, so that from space they formed a crude but obvious X. Several other land masses were scattered across the planet's shallow ocean, but they were mostly uninhabitable salt-deserts, toxic swamps or snow-fields. Almost the entire population of Tallyra – never a large number, though no one had ever bothered with anything so official as a census – lived on the four arms of the central X.

The big X, Cade thought happily. The unknown quantity, as the Edge always has been. Which is why I love it – because it's unpredictable, unconventional, ungovernable . . . And because it's *home*. Where no one will ever find me, once I've gone to ground . . .

Before long, the Starliner settled into its dock on the giant space-station, among an array of smaller vessels – freighters, probes, gypsy drifters, single-ships – scattered around it like lesser fish around a whale. The passenger transfer proceeded; the wide-bodied ferry carried them down to a bumpy landing on its patch at the spaceport where the bored port personnel waved them through with scarcely a glance. And with the usual sense of anti-climax after a long spaceflight, Cade went to register in one

35

of the main spaceport hotels, where the clerk did not seem even mildly surprised at the presence of a Brother of the Utter Dark.

Safe behind the locked door of the narrow room, Cade tossed his small shoulder-bag onto a chair and with relief pulled off the heavy black robe. It and the rest of the disguise, including a false ID, could now be dropped into a public vaporizer. The Brother would cease to exist, as if the hotel had swallowed him up.

Scratching luxuriously where the robe had itched, he gazed happily for a moment through the window at the Tallyran morning, warm in an early-summer sun. Then he glanced even more happily at the small plastic case containing the precious data-slice, safe in his bag, before stepping into the shower cubicle. Where, under the high-pressure deluge, he failed to hear the small sounds from beyond the cubicle – as the door to his room began to have its lock efficiently picked.

So the shock was like a blow, a huge blazing jolt, when he turned the shower off, stepped out of the cubicle and saw her.

The woman from the ship – the slim graceful one with the very short dark hair and the pale, dangerous-looking eyes.

She was holding up a shiny plastic disc in one hand, and Cade's heart sank as he recognized it. A PReD identification disc. Pursuit, Recovery and Delivery – an elite private force that specialized in bounty-hunting. Highly trained, highly skilled, with a galactic reputation for toughness and tenacity. Just the sort of hunter – predator – who might be sent after an escaped prisoner.

She was looking him up and down with a half-smile. 'I see you're looking yourself again. Though I didn't expect so *complete* a view.'

Cade shrugged. 'If you don't like the view, don't look.'

She laughed. 'In fact it's been interesting, watching you. You were very convincing as the old lady, getting off Breell, and you were an even better Brother.'

Cade was unable to keep from looking startled. 'You've been around all that time?'

'Most of the time,' she said, 'after I picked up your trail at Aphoz's club. Waiting for a chance to grab you quietly and privately, without any fuss – which is how I like to work.'

'I never thought Breell would go to so much trouble to get me back,' Cade said gloomily.

'Breell always thought its prison was escape-proof,' she told him, 'so they're deeply annoyed at you. And you stole a very expensive shuttle.'

Cade shrugged, studying her. He could see no sign of a weapon under her light tunic or close-fitting leggings. But the belt around her waist looked wide and thick enough to have pockets.

And he had heard about the PReD combat training, armed or unarmed. I need a distraction, he thought. But first I need to be a little less vulnerable.

'If you've seen enough,' he said lightly, 'I'll get some clothes on.'

As he spoke he took a sideways step and reached towards his bag on the chair. In the next instant, his wrist was seized in a grip like a steel clamp, his feet were swept out from under him, and he was being flung across the room to tumble helplessly onto the bed.

Sitting up, glowering as he caught his breath, he saw her rifling through the contents of his bag. 'No weapons?' she asked calmly. 'I'm surprised . . .' She tossed the bag to him. 'Right, get dressed. And try not to make any other sudden moves. I'm contracted to deliver you to Breell, but they won't care if you're not in perfect condition.'

Slowly, watchfully, Cade pulled on a plain shirt, trousers and light shoes, trying to look defeated, hoping to make her over-confident and less alert. But nothing about her changed as she watched, not the poised balance of her stance nor the unblinking watchfulness of her gaze.

'Do you have a name?' he asked. 'Or do I call you sir?'

Her mouth twitched. 'The name's Raishe

Kelme, and you might as well call me Raishe. I gather you prefer to be called Cade.'

He raised his eyebrows. 'You've done some homework on me.'

'I like to be thorough,' Raishe said. 'Not that there was much to find out. Jaxie Cade, born on Tallyra almost twenty human years ago, orphaned at the age of four, raised by a relative, showed a tendency for trouble all through childhood, left the Edge at fourteen and wandered the galaxy, often only one step ahead of the law . . .'

'Not often enough,' Cade muttered.

She smiled with mock-sympathy. 'It must be hard for you to be taken now, when you thought you were home free.'

Cade shrugged. 'I'll survive.' He studied her thoughtfully. 'Did your homework include any details about my escape from Breell?'

'There was a story about you stealing something from a Phib,' she said. 'But that's nothing to do with me . . .'

'It should be,' Cade told her, looking earnest and sincere. 'Because it might be more remarkable, and precious, than anything you can imagine.'

She frowned, but he was sure that he saw a spark of curiosity in her strange eyes. 'The only thing that would interest me,' she said, 'would be if Phibs came after you to recover the thing, and got in my way.'

It was as if the words had acted as a trigger. Without warning, the door to the room crashed open in a burst of splinters.

And through the doorway leaped a long-legged Occian, frog-mouth open in a yell, firing a small hand-weapon at Cade.

4

Collared

Sheer reflex took Cade backwards in a flailing
leap just as a tiny projectile hissed through the
place where he had been standing. As his back
slammed against the wall, and as he saw the
Phib shift position to take aim for a second shot,
he also saw something else that was nearly as
frightening.

Raishe's pale green eyes had suddenly, shock-
ingly, turned a vivid crimson.

And then she was no longer there.

It was as if she had abruptly vanished, and then
reappeared – next to the Phib, who had somehow
begun to crumple to the floor, and whose gun had
somehow got into Raishe's hand.

But as Cade found his balance and straightened, Raishe sagged back against the walls as if
suddenly grown weak, the crimson fading from
her eyes, her face pale as she fumbled at her belt.
I was right about the belt, Cade thought dazedly,
watching her take a large flat tablet from some
hidden compartment, chewing it slowly.

Almost at once colour returned to her cheeks and strength to her body. Coming upright again, she glanced out through the shattered doorway to see if anyone had been drawn to investigate the noise. But she turned, with the gun ready, when Cade took a step towards her.

He halted, half-raising his hands. 'Careful. You don't know what the Phib had in that.'

Raishe glanced down at the gun, a compact weapon called a *viper*, firing small darts that could be filled with anything from a gentle narcotic to a lethal poison. 'You almost found out the hard way,' she said, her voice strained. 'You've got good reflexes.'

'*Me?*' Cade said, remembering the inhuman crimson of her eyes, the impossible speed of her attack. 'It was *you* . . . You're *hyped*!'

She nodded, lowering the gun slightly, and Cade studied her with new interest. He had heard of the hype process, which gave people moments of almost superhuman speed and strength, but he had never seen it in action before. It seems to leave them in poor condition, he thought. Even with the viper, I might have a chance now . . .

'Have you had the hype for long?' he asked, keeping the conversation going.

'Since I became a PReD,' she replied, her mouth twisting slightly as if with a bad taste. 'The PReD high command requires what they call their *lightweight* females to have an extra edge.'

'And you don't like that,' Cade said.

She frowned. 'It's no concern of yours.'

'Fine,' he replied easily, moving another careful step towards her. 'How does the hype work? Sort of chemical?'

'In a way,' she said. 'It's an implant, into the adrenal gland. It makes a kind of super-adrenalin, giving an explosive boost of strength and speed.' She smiled faintly. 'Something like a hysterical maniac would have, or what they used to call a berserker.'

'But it takes a lot out of you,' Cade said sympathetically, easing forward another step.

Raishe nodded, touching her belt. 'That's why I carry these RePlens, replacing nutrients and energy.'

'How do you do it, though?' Cade asked, taking another step forward. 'I mean, can you just call it up when you need it?'

She shook her head. 'It's *automatic*, just as adrenalin is. I can't *summon* it. It gets triggered by fear or anger – the "fight or flight" reaction.' She gave him a mocking smile, stepping away from the wall, looking wholly restored. 'But I made top level in combat training *without* the hype, and now I have this viper. So you can stop trying to creep up on me and back off while I sort out this mess.'

Giving her a pained look, Cade backed away, while she again checked the corridor beyond the open doorway then stooped over the fallen Occian who was beginning to stir and moan. The alien wore the usual single garment of his species – a length of cloth, intricately wrapped and draped from shoulder to thigh, in the dull grey colour of the lower social classes. Swiftly and expertly Raishe searched the Occian, turning up a small metal tube covered with odd attachments and markings.

'Bio-scanner,' she said sourly. 'A bit of Phib technology we've never matched – able to pin-point a single life-form over distance.'

Cade stared at the tube with distaste. 'So this Phib was probably scanning for me at the space-port.'

She nodded, straightening. 'But at least he seems to be on his own. And now we have to move – let the hotel deal with him. I took a room on the corridor below, because I wasn't sure how quickly I'd get to you.'

She checked the corridor again, then beckoned. Obediently, Cade picked up his bag and went out, with Raishe close behind him.

'I haven't said thanks, for what you did,' Cade said as they hurried along the silent corridor.

'You're welcome,' Raishe said. 'I'm certainly not letting any other hunter take you.'

He glanced around. 'I never really expected a *Phib* hunter, here . . .'

'You should have,' she told him. 'They can read

44

the data on you too, and obviously guessed you might run to your home world. And those bio-scanners aren't fooled by ordinary disguises.'

Cade glowered. 'The disguises were just sup-posed to cover my tracks. I didn't think the Phibs would even *know* about me yet, except for the ones in the Breell jail. I don't know how they could have had one already in place on Tallyra, waiting for me.'

'In fact,' she said pointedly, 'they seem to have known about you and your theft for some while. You do know that it was a team of Phibs you escaped from in that club on Breell?'

Cade whirled to stare at her. 'I thought it was Civs . . .'

'Your old pal, Aphoz,' Raishe said ironically, 'got a better price from the Phibs. I don't know how they found out so quickly, but there were Phibs hunting you on Breell when I first got there. Whatever you took must be very precious to them.'

'To anyone,' Cade said absently, trying to absorb her unsettling news about the Occian pursuit.

'No matter,' she said briskly. 'Whatever it is, the authorities on Breell can worry about it after I hand you back to them.'

Raishe's room proved to be a replica of Cade's. Inside, she sent him to sit on a chair while she locked the door, then rummaged in her small plain holdall. Producing a portable Netlink terminal with a mini-screen, she tapped some keys. At once her face darkened with annoyance, and she half-flung the small machine back into the bag.

'*Eight days* till the next Starliner!' she stormed. 'Because of some stupid meteor showers around the Zamil system!'

'Isn't that bad luck,' Cade said with mock dismay. 'We'll be stuck here for all that time. And then we'll be together for even longer on the Starliner.' He grinned mischievously. 'Lots of time to get acquainted.'

She gave him a long cool look. 'I suppose that kind of approach, with all that boyish charm, might have some effect on young girls who don't know any better. But in fact it's really obnoxious.'

His smile tightened. 'I've always liked older women . . .' he began.

'I'm only seven years older,' she said dismissively, 'but that's not the point. Whatever creepy notions you have in mind, you can *forget* them. Is that clear?'

His smile faded completely, and he shrugged. 'All right, all right. But we still have all this time . . . What do *you* suggest we do for the next eight days? Play tourist, and see the sights of Tallyra?'

'When you'd try to disappear down the first rat-hole,' she said. 'No chance. What I'll do first is move us to a double room. Then maybe I'll just turn on the Netlink and cruise the entertainment streams.'

'You'd be brain-dead after eight days of that.' He hesitated, studying her again as if weighing her up. 'Instead, let me offer you another way to pass the time. Does your portable have a reader function?'

She blinked, then nodded and reached into her holdall for the mini-terminal. 'Why?'

He brought out the small plastic container from his own bag, removed the data-slice and held it up. 'This is what I took from the Phib on Breell. It holds what I think is a code, linked to . . . a sort of mystery.'

Still puzzled, she watched him fit the slice into the terminal. 'Why are you showing me?'

'I'm not really sure . . .' He offered a wry smile. 'I suppose I hope that if you get interested enough, you might change your mind about taking me back to Breell. If not – what do I have to lose?'

She studied him curiously. 'Careful, Cade. That was almost an honest answer . . . Let's look at your mystery, then.'

They watched in silence as the slice's odd jumble of symbols scrolled across the mini-screen. And they stared in silence at the two less jumbled lines of numerals that appeared at the end of the stream of data. Cade paused it then, watching Raishe hopefully as she frowned at those lines.

'I've seen that before,' she muttered. 'Some kind of call-sign?'

'Sort of,' Cade said. 'It's a star-chart serial number – for a very special world.'

'What world?'

He took a deep breath. 'The one that's usually called the Phantom Planet.'

She gazed at him for a moment, her frown clearing, and then burst into laughter. 'You can't mean that!' she said. 'The Phantom Planet . . . It's a *myth*!'

'It's not,' Cade told her fiercely. 'Not to people here on the Edge, anyway. We *know* it's out there. And there's never been an Edger who hasn't dreamed of being the one to find it.'

'Are you serious?' she demanded. 'Or is this some kind of trick?'

He sighed. 'Try to forget about the junk stories on the Net about the Phantom Planet. Beyond all that, the Planet is real and true.'

Then he told her the story that every native Edger knew. About the ship with a faulty drive that drifted past Tallyra and out into the Deeps beyond the galactic Edge. Where, to that crew's astonishment, a small rogue planet, or planet-oid, appeared on the ship's screens. It was a

48

dead world, nothing but rock and dust, spinning slowly in total isolation. But as the ship with the faulty drive drifted towards it, the lone planetoid suddenly displayed a weird shimmering glow – and disappeared.

Raishe grinned. 'Evil sorcery, I suppose.'

Ignoring the comment, Cade went on, relating how the damaged ship's drive failed completely as it tried to limp back towards Tallyra. The powerless ship crashed on one of Tallyra's empty sister-worlds, killing the crew and scattering fragments over a considerable area. But when a team from Tallyra went to clear up the mess and bring away the dead, it also retrieved some part of the ship's data-store, more or less intact.

And in that data-store was a clear record of the solitary planetoid, drifting out beyond the Edge, and its uncanny disappearance.

But also, the data-store held the results of a preliminary sweep-survey of the planetoid, made automatically by the ship's sensors. And it revealed that the planetoid was incredibly, bountifully rich in the galaxy's rarest and most precious substance – spallerium, the weirdly crystallized pseudo-metal that was the crucial element in forming the spin-drive field, which made interstellar travel possible.

Raishe wore a mocking smile, although her eyes held a glint of bright interest. 'It's like the ancient stories of buried treasure. The sort of thing that tricksters like you do fake *maps* of, to sell to fools.'

'Not at all,' Cade said. 'A lot of people have seen that data from the crashed ship. And other people have claimed to have seen the Phantom Planet itself, since then – at different locations.'

Raishe laughed. 'So the legend goes on growing, like a fungus.'

'Maybe,' Cade said coolly. 'But most star charts give the planet a notional position, beyond the Edge, and a serial number – the one on this slice.' He gestured at the screen. 'And the Phib who had the slice, in prison, kept saying that it was "worth the price of a world".'

Raishe nibbled her lip thoughtfully. 'I wonder . . . Those Phibs coming after you on Breell made me curious, so I did some checking – on the one in prison with you. He was a specialist *tech-thief*, did you know? Wanted on a lot of worlds. Though he was jailed on Breell after his single-ship broke down and he tried to get away without paying for the repairs.'

'So he could have stolen the slice from somewhere else, before he got to Breell,' Cade said intently. 'And he found out that it says something about the Phantom Planet. He might even have broken the code, if it is a code, on the rest of the slice.'

She chewed her lip again. 'I think it must be

a code. And we might try breaking it, too. Even if we don't have any proper facilities . . .' She stopped, seeing Cade's grin. 'What?'

'*We*,' he said. 'You're saying *we*.'

She made a face. 'Don't jump to any conclusions. I'm just playing your game.' She peered at the screen again. 'Anyway, even supposing this Phantom Planet is real and you could break the code and find it – what do you imagine you'd *do* with it? Set up your own planetary mining company?'

Cade frowned. 'I haven't really thought that far ahead. I'd have to file some kind of claim . . . Lease the mining rights, or something . . .'

'Dream on,' she said mockingly. 'Before then, some very dangerous folk would have filleted you and grabbed the spallerium for themselves. You should really be *glad* that I'm taking you back to a nice safe jail.'

'Not for eight days,' Cade reminded her. 'And I could get some help, here on Tallyra, to crack the code in a few *hours*.' He smiled his most cajoling smile. 'I'd just need to *talk* to someone.'

She laughed, though the bright gleam of interest remained visible in her eyes. 'And I imagine the person you want to talk to is the person who raised you, your *uncle*, Eyr Graklin, known as the Datamaster – one of the most notorious criminals in the Commonwealth. Just the man to arrange a little getaway.'

For a moment Cade looked crestfallen. 'Actually he's my *great*-uncle. And he has never been convicted of any crime.'

'Which doesn't mean he hasn't committed any,' she replied.

'That's not the point,' Cade said earnestly. 'He could help, Raishe – with the code. He can do anything with info-tech, better than anyone in the galaxy.' He touched her arm, looking sincere. 'I'm not thinking about prison or escape right now. I'm thinking about the next eight days that we have to spend on Tallyra. And I'm thinking about solving a mystery, and maybe finding the most valuable planetoid ever known.'

'What *I'm* thinking about is my contract with Breell,' she replied.

He squeezed her arm gently. 'What's that worth, compared to the Planet? In fact, what's your whole job as a PReD worth – when you don't seem happy in it anyway?'

She frowned, not replying at once, looking thoughtful. 'Out of curiosity, where is your great-uncle?'

'In Tallyra's main city, Sewr Beic, ' Cade said.

'The Sewer,' she said, grimacing. 'Where I'm sure you know every alley and hideaway.'

'Raishe,' he said, shaking his head. 'How could I get away from a hyped PReD with a viper? I'd be crazy to try!'

'Yes, you would,' she agreed, going to search in

52

her bag again, 'and even crazier once you've put this on.' She straightened, holding out a dangling metal band with decorative inlays.

'What is it?' Cade asked suspiciously.

'A restraining collar,' she said, 'designed to look like a necklet. If you get more than twenty metres from me with it on, or if you try to remove it, it injects a narco-drug into your throat that knocks you out till I give you the antidote.' She held it up insistently. 'Wear this, Cade, and I'll consider taking you to see your great-uncle.'

He scowled at the collar for several silent moments, then shrugged. 'If that's how it has to be.'

'It is,' she told him, leaning close to fasten the collar around his neck, staring into his eyes. 'And I hope I don't regret this. But just remember, Cade – if you do find a way to run, I'll come after you. And I'll find you again, as I did before, wherever you hide.'

'If you say so,' he said, smiling.

She drew back with a sigh. 'Maybe there's something in the air, on the Edge, that makes people break the rules.'

'Rules?' Cade echoed brightly. 'What rules?'

Her pale eyes grew fierce. '*My* rules, for you, right now. And the first one for you to remember is that whatever you hope to do on Tallyra – find a mythical planet, visit relatives, play hide-and-seek with Phibs – you have only *eight days* to do it in.'

53

5

Sewr Beic

They paused in one of the hotel's eateries for a light midday meal, during which Raishe watched Cade unwaveringly, as if she expected him to run at any moment. At the same time, her expression seemed slightly surprised – as if she still could not wholly believe that she had let herself be talked into wandering around Tallyra with someone supposedly her prisoner.

But Cade kept up a flow of chatty conversation, trying to relax and reassure her, to keep her from changing her mind. After the meal, they collected one of the narrow city-cars that the hotel rented to customers. And as they sped away from the spaceport – with Cade driving, since he knew the way – he was still talking, telling Raishe about Tallyra.

They were moving towards the centre, where the Four Bridges linked the four populated land masses of the X. The different segments of the X, Cade explained, had grand, formal, official names, but no Tallyran ever used them. Instead, the directions in which the land masses lay had given them short, popular nicknames – Nen, Sen, En and Wen.

The massive complex of the spaceport was on Nen, with most businesses concerned with space travel, import-export and so on – along with much heavy industry and many good-sized towns housing the employees of all those enterprises. The land mass called En held many more towns and small cities full of research and tech facilities, financial centres, colleges and the like, surrounded by satellite suburbs and light-industry complexes. And the land mass known as Sen was different again: mostly agricultural, with only small towns and villages scattered over its fertile plains and hills, along with some lush private estates and most of Tallyra's hospitals and polyclinics.

But the fourth and largest land mass – Wen, where Cade and Raishe were heading – was the most different of the four.

Wen was primarily Tallyra's playground. Its further end boasted lakes and rivers, snow-capped mountains and long scenic beaches, offering most sorts of outdoor fun. And the flatlands of the centre held a huge range of sporting arenas, race-tracks, fairgrounds, pan-galactic zoos and public gardens, with activities and recreations designed to attract visitors from any of a million worlds. There you could find most games, from cube-chess to rifle-ball, and with them many other pastimes that were outlawed on most human worlds. So you could watch fighting stone-dragons from the planet Eledd, you could hunt mammoth killer-sloths from the Ikannil system, you could watch or bet on or take part in a wide range of human combat or pursuit, armed or unarmed, often to the death.

But the fact was – as Cade told Raishe with a grin – that by far the largest majority of fun-seeking visitors to Wen never managed to get to the centre of that land mass, nor to its farther end. Because the idea of *fun* for most visitors was more, in Cade's words, sin and sleaze.

And for those attractions, no one had to go much farther than the end of the bridge on to Wen – which led directly into the planet's primary city, Sewr Beic, known to everyone as the Sewer.

In fact, the city of Sewr Beic looked less like a sewer than like a cesspool. Its densely populated heart lay in the depths of an enormous basin from which it expanded up on to the surrounding slopes in a wholly unplanned fashion. It was indeed no more than a sprawl, looking from above like a colossal ink-blot on crumpled paper with secondary dribbles and smears extending all around. And the ink-blot comparison was quite apt, since the city was never truly itself until after dark, when the night-life of the Sewer swung into action.

In those nights, the name of the game was pleasure – unaffected by any concerns of morality or good taste, seldom restrained by the Civil Patrol unless there was a danger of upsetting the tourists. In the Sewer, Cade told Raishe happily, you could more or less do anything and get anything – no matter how illegal, immoral or threatening – that you could imagine wanting.

'In fact,' Cade went on, 'that's the only *real* limit on what people can get up to in the Sewer. Their own imaginations – what they can dream of *wanting* to do. Because if you can think of it, you can most likely find it, here.'

Raishe's mouth and posture had tightened a little during his account of the joys of Sewr Beic. But part of that, as they drew closer to the mighty bridge that linked the two land masses of Nen and Wen, may have been due to Cade's driving. He was familiar with the car, and highly skilled – but Tallyran roads seemed to have no restrictions, including speed limits, and Cade clearly relished the challenge of driving as fast as possible in among hordes of other vehicles doing exactly the same. And he was glancing at Raishe as they went, grinning at her tension, which made her even more annoyed and tense.

But then the bridge itself was enough to dismay any newcomer. It and the other three bridges were magno-grav structures, relying on forces drawn from the planetary core. So the immense arch, growing ever nearer as the little car hurtled on, rose high into the Tallyran sky with absolutely no visible means of support.

As they went on, Raishe was unable to get an advance look at Sewr Beic even if she had wanted one, since the bridge was some forty kilometres long and a leftover mist was drifting over the shallow turquoise sea below it. But also, the Sewer did not offer a long-range view of itself, for it had none of the soaring, sky-scraping towers and spires that adorned major cities on other human worlds. Instead, Sewr Beic – especially in its central basin – was a place of low, dark, cramped buildings huddled along narrow streets and an unbelievable network of alleys, lanes, courts, paths, trails, tunnels, ramps, foot-bridges, flyovers and secret passages. It was a tangle, a maze, a labyrinth like almost no other in the Commonwealth, where anyone might get lost anytime – tourists by accident, criminals or fugitives on purpose . . .

'And you love it, don't you,' Raishe said to Cade in reply to his last remark. 'It's just your sort of place.'

He glanced at her, grinning again at the dis-approval in her voice and her expression. 'It's home,' he replied. 'Where I was born and raised. Lots of people have fond feelings about their home.'

She was silent for a moment, as if regretting

having revealed her distaste. 'The data on you,' she said at last, 'said your parents were killed in an accident.'

Cade nodded. 'They were techs at the spaceport who got caught in a ship burn-out. I don't remember them very well.'

'And Eyr Graklin took you in – the kindly great-uncle,' Raishe said sarcastically. 'And introduced you to a life of crime.'

'You've got him wrong,' Cade told her. 'He's not a gangster – he's never done armed robbery or kidnapping or any really hard crime. He began as a *provider*, buying and selling . . .'

'Providing weapons and other criminal hardware,' Raishe interrupted, 'handling stolen goods and embezzled funds, acting as a consultant for major fraud . . .'

'And then,' Cade said with an untroubled nod, 'he began to specialize in *information*. Which of course is now his main thing. He's become the galaxy's greatest hacker – the Datamaster. He designs his own special systems, and he's able to access the data-fields of more worlds than I can count, tapping into the Net-streams across the galaxy. He mostly stays away from Phib worlds, because they can get nasty, but there aren't many data-stores and info-memories in the Commonwealth, maybe the Aggregation too, that he can't get into.'

'Illegally,' Raishe said.

Cade shrugged. 'I suppose. I never said he was law-abiding. But he's not a violent criminal, he doesn't deal in drugs or sleaze or cruelty . . . And he was always good to me.'

'Made you what you are today,' Raishe said dryly.

He laughed. 'Not entirely. I did some of that myself.'

By then the car was humming up along the approach road that led on to the bridge, which looked even more unnerving from so close, its massive swooping curve seeming to be held up by nothing more substantial than the ragged remains of the mist. After pausing to pay a toll, they climbed smoothly on up the incline, where other roads also led on to the bridge, bringing a huge flood of traffic – city-cars and robo-cabs, giant road-trains on auto-guidance, multi-wheeled commercial vehicles, one-person micros, segmented flexi-buses . . . Cade fell silent, then, concentrating on his driving – though seeming to feel no need to reduce speed, flashing and weaving through the traffic with an exhilarated smile while Raishe was tending to close her eyes and hold her breath.

Soon the car swept up over the top of the arch and hurtled, roller-coaster style, down the far slope. By then the closely packed clutter and mazy tangle of Sewr Beic had become visible, and as they sped off the bridge and into the city

Raishe stared out with an expression of unease at the winding, interweaving, shapeless muddle of the roadways, their narrow griminess alight with garish invitations and promises glaring from the front of nearly every building, the walk-ways crowded with fun-seekers even then in the mid-afternoon. Yet Cade sent the car whisking through the labyrinth of those back streets and alleys as if he had a detailed map in front of him – which clearly made Raishe even more uneasy.

After a further time, when they had bypassed the edge of the central basin and climbed partway up a steep street in a more residential area, the car slid to a stop in front of the last building in the street. It was a tall, square, imposing house, all in solid syntho-wood and native stone, with blank polarized windows and what looked like a reinforced metal door.

'Quite a fortress,' Raishe said. 'Is it Graklin's home or HQ?'

'Both,' Cade told her. 'He doesn't go out much. He has a disability, a breakdown in the bones of his legs. He hasn't walked for years.'

Raishe blinked. 'I didn't know that . . . But all the same, Cade, don't forget what I said before. If you and your uncle try anything to get you away from me, I might drop you with the viper before the collar gets you.' She touched her belt where she had stowed the Occian gun. 'I'm a good shot – and we still don't know what that Phib was using in his darts.'

'Stop fretting,' Cade said easily. 'I know when I'm beaten. Let's just go and see Uncle Grak.'

She peered at him. 'You really *do* want to go in there and tell a super-crook, who specializes in information, all about your precious data-slice?'

'Absolutely,' Cade said without hesitation. 'I trust him. And he has what I need – what *we* need – to crack that code.' He grinned cheerfully. 'And to help us make a fortune from the Phantom Planet, when we find it.'

At more or less the same time (in interstellar terms), within a building in the main core-city on the Heartworld of the Occian Unity, two Occians were in consultation. The wrapping of one of them – the knee-length garment, intricately draped – was stark black with a small ornament at the throat. And that Occian was clearly deferring to the other, an older individual in a high-necked wrapping of brilliant green with a much larger ornament. They were in the older one's chamber, high in the building's bulging upper dome, surmounting a low tower like a stem, all part of the Heartworld's Central Rulership complex.

More specifically, the building was a nerve-centre of the espionage branch of the Occian military – of which the older one in green was an Overseer and the younger one in black merely a Troop-handler.

If an Occian could be capable of any emotions more powerful than generalized malice and cold-blooded hunger, the green-clad Overseer might have been furious and the Troop-handler fearful. But since they were Occians, the conversation remained flat, toneless, chillingly composed.

'It has become a catalogue of failure,' the Overseer rasped, baring his serrated teeth. 'He who first acquired the data-slice failed to bring it to us at once, then was imprisoned. Those sent to Breell to await his release were thwarted by the human thief, then failed to block his escape. And now your agent, Troop-handler, has failed on Tallyra.'

Membranes slid as if nervously up and down over the Troop-handler's lizard eyes. 'The human woman who first contacted the thief appears to be one of the hunter group known as PReDs, and is unusually skilled. But our agent did at least *locate* the thief, Overseer.'

'That is so,' the older Occian conceded. 'And that is why you remain in your position, Troop-handler. Although I question the wisdom of sending only one agent to watch for the thief in his home world.'

'I had been considering the cost, Overseer. Even a small ship, to the galactic Edge . . . But I now have a further two agents already in place on Tallyra, seeking the thief – and a larger team in readiness if required.'

The Overseer's wrinkled throat swelled. 'Very well. But I expect no more failures. Bear in mind, Troop-handler, that the human thief stole a priceless object, and also in doing so committed an offence against the Unity. The Rulership wishes that object to be retrieved, and the thief punished. No expense is to be spared in that effort. And no one will escape judgment, Troop-handler, if their folly or incompetence prevents its success.'

The Datamaster

'. . . so I had to find a ship out of that system in a hurry,' Cade said. He had been telling an involved tale of an earlier adventure, before the one that had got him imprisoned. 'With an Illiyan fraud squad breathing down my neck.'

Eyr Graklin chuckled, glancing over at Raishe to share his amusement. He was a small, pale, old man with a cloud of white hair around a bald pate and twinkling eyes set deep in a round wrinkled face. He looked kindly, slightly vague and quite harmless – especially since he was confined with his legs covered to a gleaming servo-chair, floating on magnos a few centimetres above the floor of the airy, comfortably furnished room. But he seemed mobile enough in the high-tech chair. And he also seemed to be well looked after, by several servants – or bodyguards – including the hard-faced man who had admitted Cade and Raishe, and the watchful woman who had brought their drinks.

Graklin had seemed genuinely delighted by

the unexpected arrival of his great-nephew. And both of them seemed wholly genuine in their affectionate manner towards one another. But Raishe sat apart from the two of them, her expression still mingling wariness with faint disbelief, as if she could not quite understand how she had come to be a guest in the home of the Datamaster – a man known to every law-enforcement agency in the Human Commonwealth – in the company of an escaped convict.

'That's the trouble with having to run empty-handed,' Graklin was saying, commenting on Cade's story. 'You become incautious. So you landed on Breell, needing money, working with that snake Aphoz – and ended up in prison.'

Cade shrugged. 'So it goes. I'll deal with Aphoz one day.'

'He sold you to the Phibs,' Raishe put in, 'but he didn't deliver you. I think the Phibs will deal with him.'

Graklin nodded, then sighed. 'If only you had come to me, Jaxie . . . You would have avoided so much discomfort. Really, I do think you ought to have put an end to this frivolous, footloose, *insecure* life of yours by now. Open a new chapter, here on Tallyra where you belong. You know I've always hoped that you'd come home to stay, to work alongside me . . .'

Cade grinned. 'I know, Uncle Grak. But I'm

not ready for that kind of new chapter just yet. I've still got a galaxy full of places to go, people to see, fun to find . . .'

'Not till Breell lets you out of jail,' Raishe said pointedly.

'Quite so,' Graklin said with another sigh. 'Perhaps a term in prison will change your mind about all that *fun* . . . But now – what is this present enterprise, that brought an Occian hunting you?'

They all looked down at the small plastic case that lay innocuously on the polished table beside Graklin's chair. 'The data-slice holds a code that needs cracking,' Cade said. 'With other data that might surprise you. And I'd be grateful, Grak, if you could keep it to yourself.'

Raishe made a sound like a delicate snort, but neither of them looked her way.

'Of course, of course.' The older man frowned. 'If the first Occian, the one who had the slice in prison, was right about what he thought it was worth . . . Are you sure you understood him correctly, Jaxie?'

That brought Raishe upright, startled. 'That never even entered my mind!' she said. 'Of course, that Phib would have used his own language when he talked about "the price of a world" . . . And *you* speak it, Cade?'

'I understand it better than I speak it,' Cade said. 'I did a speed course – hypno-learning.'

'All part of the education that I insisted he should have,' Graklin said proudly.

'What else did he study?' Raishe asked acidly. 'Advanced thievery?'

The old man smiled. 'He had a fairly normal education, when he could be persuaded to attend classes. I did also insist that he should study other worlds and their ways – that he should know how to handle a wide range of vehicles – and of course that he should learn as much as possible about info-tech and the data-fabric. For which he has some flair, perhaps inherited.' He chuckled proudly. 'All to equip him for life in an often hostile galaxy.'

'To equip him for life as an outlaw,' Raishe muttered.

'Can we get back to the slice?' Cade asked impatiently.

Still smiling merrily, Graklin reached for the plastic case. 'I'll be intrigued to see the data it carries, and its code. But breaking the code will take some time.'

'How long?' Cade asked. 'Remember, Raishe has put sort of a time limit on things.'

'Indeed,' Graklin said. 'But first of all I'll need to work out the language or data-base that provides the references for the code. Only then will I be able to begin de-coding. And I won't have any idea of the time-scale until I've studied the slice.' He paused, considering. 'Do you have somewhere secure to stay?'

Cade grimaced. 'Where's secure? We're in a spaceport hotel at the moment – but if one Phib could find me there, others could, too . . .'

'They'd still have to get past me,' Raishe told him, 'as long as you're my prisoner.'

'You're welcome to stay here, of course,' Graklin said. 'I have plenty of room.'

'No, thanks,' she said at once. 'Cade will need some watching on his own, even with the collar. Staying here, I'd never be able to relax for a second, wondering what you *both* were up to.'

Graklin laughed. 'I quite understand. But even so, I hope you won't reject my help. I own a little place near the Bridge, which shows no connection to me in any Tallyran data-store. It's a well-protected apartment in a building with adequate security, and it's yours for as long as you want it.'

'Thanks, Uncle Grak,' Cade said gratefully. 'That sounds just what we need.'

'It sounds almost *too* good,' Raishe said suspiciously. 'If this is part of some sneaky escape trick, you can forget it.'

'Not at all,' Graklin assured her. 'I keep the place as a temporary hideaway, in case of any . . . difficulties. A man in my line of work can make enemies . . .' He gestured vaguely, smiling at Raishe. 'I'm planning no tricks, believe me. In

69

any case, I don't imagine anyone would find it easy to escape from you, my dear.'

'Cade won't, anyway, I can promise you,' Raishe said flatly. 'And, Mr Graklin – call me Raishe, or whatever, but I'm *not* your dear.'

Cade burst out laughing. 'Careful, Grak. She doesn't have a lot of time for us nasty criminals . . . Anyway, *I'm* grateful for the use of your hideaway. And we might as well go and get settled. I'll call you later, when you've had a first look at the slice.'

So they took their leave, retracing their route to the spaceport hotel in near-silence. Cade was focused on his driving, though still quite unconcerned with speed limits within the even denser late-afternoon traffic. And Raishe seemed lost in thought – frowning as if she was still wondering what she had let herself in for, and how she could have chosen to do so.

At the hotel they remained mostly silent, watchful and alert. But they saw no sign of Occians anywhere, and no one in the hotel seemed at all interested in them. Not when the whole place was still buzzing with rumours and gossip about the injured Phib discovered in the room of a Brother of the Utter Dark, who had disappeared without paying his bill.

After Raishe checked out, they took an anonymous robo-copter back into the city, and from its landing station hailed a ground-cab, also on auto-guidance, to the address Graklin had given them. It was a square, solid, stone-built block where some square, solid security men glowered at the key-card Cade had been given and reluctantly let them in. The apartment that was Graklin's 'hideaway' was in the centre of the building, with reinforced doors and windows and a complex alarm system. And its compact design included two bedrooms, to Cade's mock-regret.

While Cade prowled, looking the place over, Raishe went to stare glumly out of the window. By then night had fallen, and the cloudless sky was offering one of the special features of the planet known as the Edge-world. Tallyra's rotation had brought the city on to the side of the planet that faced out towards what Edgers called the Deeps – the unimaginable immensity of space extending beyond the galaxy. Of course it was by no means wholly unoccupied or lightless space, yet it was not nearly as brilliantly star-crowded a night sky as an inner world would offer. In the near distance a few wandering asteroids and other unattached bodies showed small points of light, as did one of Tallyra's two lifeless sister planets. But beyond them, the Deeps revealed little more than scattered spots and clumps and shapeless smudges of brightness, which could have been constellation clusters, nebulae or entire galaxies.

'Trying to spot the Phantom Planet?' Cade said teasingly, coming up beside her.

She sniffed, touching the tab that closed the protective flexi-metal curtains. 'I'll leave that dream to you and your great-uncle.'

'Really?' He laughed. 'It seems to me you've been caught up by that dream as much as anyone. Why don't you admit it?'

She frowned, turning away. 'All right – maybe I have got *interested*. I like a good mystery . . . and the Planet probably appeals to a get-rich-quick urge in most people . . .'

'Especially people who don't like their lives the way they are,' Cade broke in, smiling.

'Don't make too much of that, Cade,' she said sharply. 'I enjoy being a PReD, and I'm good at it.'

'But you have trouble with the high command, you said,' Cade replied.

Her mouth tightened. 'Of sorts. There seems to be a *barrier* that the younger female PReDs run up against. Maybe male prejudice or something. So I get nudged aside into the minor, less well-paid scruff jobs – like chasing small-time tricksters turned fugitive.' She looked pointedly at him. 'And I suppose I don't really see things getting any better for me.'

'So the Phantom Planet . . .' Cade began.

'So the Phantom Planet,' she interrupted, 'is nice to *dream* about. And it's an intriguing puzzle, and a bit of excitement – which all helps to make things interesting for a while. Until we get back to real life, when the Starliner docks a few days from now.'

That reminder created another silence, as they occupied themselves with an evening meal. The apartment was well enough supplied, they found, though Cade was not pleased with the ready-made and semi-tasteless dinner packs. He was even less pleased with the available entertainment on the Netlink screen – while Raishe, after briefly and idly cruising the screen streams, disappeared into one of the bedrooms, with a last reminder about the restraining collar's twenty-metre range, and the viper-gun that would be at her fingertips all night.

For a while after her door closed, Cade glared into a mirror at the collar around his neck, trying to think of a safe way to remove it. But none came to mind, and so he wheeled restlessly away, wanting to call Graklin on the Netlink, knowing that it would be too pointlessly soon to do so. He paced awhile, his mind a clutter of half-formed ideas and impulses, dominated by the thought of the definite interest that Raishe had begun to show in the possibilities of the Phantom Planet. Which was his best hope, perhaps his only hope, of staying out of jail . . .

The morning brought Cade little relief from restlessness and vexation. He called Graklin, only to be told that the old man was working and could not be disturbed. The Netlink's entertainment offerings were still as pathetic, the food-packs as unappealing. And Raishe had again withdrawn into a cool, watchful silence, except for one or two pointed reminders that the Starliner was getting closer every moment. So that entire day drifted past, uneventfully, emptily, inconclusively.

And so in exactly the same way most of the *next* day passed – with Cade's fretful uneasiness winding him tighter and tighter.

Until Graklin called, just after sunset, to offer a crumb of hope.

'I may have had a breakthrough, Jax,' the old man said. 'I'll say no more on the Netlink, and anyway I need more time. But if you two can come here about mid-afternoon tomorrow, there may be some news. I keep a city-car in the underground garage, there, that you can use . . .'

Babbling excited thanks, Cade switched off, whirling towards Raishe so joyfully that she backed warily away. But when he told her, she seemed relieved as well, as if she too had been growing tense and troubled in their isolation.

'What do you say?' Cade asked her, then, with a hopeful smile. 'Could a prisoner and his custodian go out tonight to celebrate – with a drink and some *proper* food? I know a place I think you'd like . . .'

The prospect of the food seemed to tip the

74

balance. Raishe accepted, after further warnings about escape attempts and any other foolishness. The car in the underground garage was readily unlocked with the apartment key-card, and Cade again did the driving, at his usual hectic pace. The destination turned out to be a cosy bar and eatery that offered almost no suggestions of the Sewer's normal night-life, aside from occasional screams from the street. And during the meal Cade did everything he could to overcome Raishe's wariness and put her at ease, so that when they were driving home at the end of the evening they were both feeling far more relaxed than they had the previous night.

Perhaps that was why, at first, they failed to notice the two dark figures riding the narrow, powerful alley-bike, following them at some distance through the traffic. But they definitely did notice when, as they drove into the dim basement garage of their building, the alley-bike came in after them.

And a glimmer of light in the garage's dimness showed the wide mouths and bulging lizard eyes of the bike's Occian riders.

7

Mysteries

'Phibs!' Cade yelled as the bike surged towards them, a viper-gun glinting in the hand of the Occian riding pillion.

But even before he began to change direction, Raishe's hand flickered, and suddenly she was firing her own viper from the car window. As the bike swerved to avoid the shot, Cade dragged the car into a screeching turn and sent it hurtling back towards the exit ramp.

Raishe braced herself as they flashed back up the ramp and out on to the street. But there Cade spun the car into another howling, skidding turn, all the way around, and then gave it full power – back the way they had come. And Raishe had only begun to look startled when they blasted back down onto the ramp, and met the pursuing alley-bike head on.

The Occian driver was quick enough to start evasive action, so the car hit the bike only a glancing blow. Even so, the bike was flung aside, bouncing off the wall and crashing down the ramp. As it came to a sliding, spinning, grinding halt, Cade hit his brakes to halt the car and Raishe leaped out with gun ready. But there was no need, for both Occians lay crumpled and stunned beyond the wrecked bike.

Raishe exhaled slowly, turning as Cade came out to join her. 'You take a few chances, don't you?' she said sourly.

'It seemed better than being chased around the city,' he said with a shrug, then scowled at the aliens. 'I just wonder how many *more* Phibs are on Tallyra, after me.'

'With bio-scanners,' she reminded him, 'so they'll find you as easily as these did.'

He nodded unhappily, glancing around the shadowed garage. 'We'd better keep moving, then. Anyway, this mess will stir up security before long, maybe even the Civs.'

'Let's hope,' she said as they turned back to the car, 'that we don't run out of places to stay before we run out of Phibs.'

'Not on Tallyra,' Cade assured her. 'We can go to a short-stay inn for tonight, and tomorrow I'll ask Grak to find us another place.' He offered a crooked smile. 'Another cosy hideaway for us, until the Starliner arrives to take me to jail. Unless you've changed your mind . . .?'

'Don't get your hopes up,' she told him firmly. 'Not *any* of them.'

*   *   *

77

At roughly the same time, on a world in a planetary system at the heart of the far-flung Human Commonwealth, a section chief of the Commonwealth's top intelligence agency was meeting with his commander. Both were lean, fit, tidily dressed, tough and capable-looking, although the grey-haired commander was smaller, older, and female. And both were gazing fixedly at a three-dimensional holo-globe that was showing the visuals of the section chief's report.

One of the agency's primary tasks lay in keeping a close watch on humankind's hostile rivals, the Occian Unity. And the section chief had picked up some intriguing hints regarding some unusual, and unusually *distant*, Occian activity.

'You don't get Phibs on the Edge much,' the chief growled. 'So when one turns up hurt in a spaceport hotel room, it gets noticed.'

The commander nodded, studying a group of faces that had appeared on the holo. 'And you link the incident with these Starliner passengers?'

'It's a good probability.' The chief adjusted the holo to focus on one of the faces – Cade's face, covered in the black make-up of his disguise. 'This one, one of the Brothers of the Utter Dark, had the room where the Phib was found. And he *hasn't* been found.'

'I don't expect the Civil Patrol on Tallyra looked very hard,' the commander said dryly.

'You know the Edge,' the chief agreed. 'All very rough and ready, and the Civs there don't overwork themselves. Anyway, we've picked up indications of a lot of Phib interest in Tallyra. And, meanwhile, one of our contacts in another sector heard something about a human convict escaping from a planet called Breell, who's thought to have snatched some mysterious thing that the Phibs put a high value on. This is him.'

Cade's normal face appeared on the holo, a stiff glum image clearly taken for prison records. Then the chief shifted the visuals so that the blackened face of the Brother was superimposed over Cade's.

The commander raised her eyebrows. 'Same person?'

'Definitely,' the chief said. 'Jaxie Cade, a small-time trickster and outlaw, born and bred on Tallyra. Who is apparently the great-nephew of – guess who. Eyr Graklin.'

The commander's eyebrows rose higher. 'The Datamaster? *He's* involved in this?'

'Seems so,' the chief confirmed. 'Anyway, this Cade is back on the Edge, probably carrying something that the Phibs are trying to retrieve.'

The commander pursed her lips. 'Let's hope young Cade can hang on to it. Long enough for us to find out what the thing is – and to find a way to grab it for *ourselves*. Do we have a good agent on the Edge?'

'We have an *agent*,' the chief said carefully. The holo stirred again, showing the face of an almost classically handsome man – thick blond hair, chiselled cheekbones, shining white teeth, strong dimpled chin. 'Hyrd Hempel,' the chief grunted. 'Our man on Tallyra.'

'You don't approve?' asked the commander.

The chief shrugged. 'We had a good person there, but she retired. Hempel is just filling in till a senior agent takes over. He's a junior, fairly new and *very* gung-ho – but I don't know how good he is.'

'Still, he's all we've got,' the commander said calmly. 'So send him a coded flash, over a high-speed priority relay. Tell him to find this Cade, and watch him.' Her mouth curved in a dry smile. 'And tell him not to do anything rash till we can get some back-up to Tallyra.'

'It's most upsetting,' Eyr Graklin said, shaking his white-rimmed head sadly. The three of them were together again in the old man's reception room, where Cade had given a very brief account of the previous night's adventure. 'Occians attacking humans on Tallyra . . . Perhaps I should provide you with a bodyguard.'

'To watch over us, or just *watch* us?' Raishe asked stonily.

Graklin looked sorrowful. 'Jax, I believe Raishe is still feeling suspicious about me.'

'She's a PReD,' Cade said idly. 'She can't help it.'

Graklin sighed, shaking his head. 'Meanwhile, Jaxie,' he said sadly, 'as long as you have the data-slice, you'll continue to be in danger. I doubt if the Occians will give up the hunt. And by now rumours will surely be spreading, through the human worlds and elsewhere, about a priceless piece of information taken from a jail on Breell.'

'That's true enough,' Raishe agreed. 'The news is bound to have got out. Every hijacker and cutthroat in the galaxy will be on your trail, Cade, as the word spreads.'

Cade grimaced. 'Then we'd better leave less of a trail.'

'And you must hope,' Graklin said sombrely, 'that the rumours don't include the fact that the data you have concerns the Phantom Planet – and how it can be located.'

'Grak!' Cade cried, leaping to his feet. 'You've cracked the code!'

'I have – more or less, and not without difficulty.' Graklin's face clouded. 'But you may not be pleased by the result.'

'Why not?' Cade demanded. 'What does it say?'

'It says a great deal,' Graklin replied, 'but not enough. It solves some of the mystery of the Phantom Planet, but then imposes new mysteries

81

on to it.' He sighed, then beckoned. 'You'd best come and see.'

They followed his floating servo-chair out of the room, up the stairs, and into an isolated and completely different chamber. It was an enormous tech facility, crammed full yet neatly arranged, with its cabinets and tables holding a variety of Netlink terminals and info-structures, along with other consoles and data stores, stacks of readers, scanners and other peripherals, every sort of state-of-the-art information technology that would be needed to penetrate not only any planet's data-field but the entire galaxy's data-fabric.

Raishe stared around, looking almost awed – aware that she had entered the nerve centre where the notorious Datamaster wove his far-flung webs. And Cade watched her, grinning.

'You're privileged,' Cade told her. 'This is the sanctum – Uncle Grak's most private place.' He gestured at the arrays of equipment. 'Lots of this stuff is top secret, because Grak designed and built it himself. He doesn't let many people in here.'

'Perhaps I trust Raishe more than she trusts me,' Graklin murmured.

Closing the door carefully, the old man touched a button that put the hazy shimmer of a privacy shield over the windowless walls and doorway, then went to switch on one of the poly-function systems. Gathering around, they watched as the jumbled symbols stored on the data-slice appeared on one side of the screen, and their decoded translation on the other.

'Looks like more code,' Raishe said, frowning.

'It's guidance data for a spaceship computer,' Cade said, watching intently as the symbols slowly scrolled past. 'Plotting a route to intersect with the Phantom Planet . . .' Then he halted, stiffening, glaring at the screen with anger and astonishment. 'What *is* all this? An *AI*? And a *Fse*?'

'So it seems,' Graklin said. 'I doubt if that's an error, although the code was uncommonly difficult to unravel. Indeed, I suspect that the code was itself devised by a non-organic brain.' He gestured at the screen. 'And, as you see, this data says that the Phantom Planet's path – its random, erratic movements and almost magical disappearances – have been *tracked*, and plotted. By an Artificial Intelligence.'

Cade scowled. 'There aren't supposed to be any of those any more.'

'Exactly,' Graklin agreed. 'So we have a new mystery. Or more than one.'

'It's more than a mystery,' Raishe said, frowning at the screen. 'It's ridiculous. An Artificial Intelligence that can't exist is showing how to find a Phantom Planet that has to be a myth . . .'

'You may be right to be sceptical,' Graklin said mildly. 'I wondered at first if the data-slice might have been assembled a long time ago, by an AI that existed then. But in fact it seems to be much more recent.' He sighed. 'It would have helped to know more about the slice – including where the Occian data-thief first stole it from. But so far I've found no record anywhere of such a theft.'

'I bet that Phib told his masters in the Unity, though,' Cade growled unhappily. 'And now we've got this *Fse* in it as well . . .'

'Another mystery,' Graklin said. 'The guidance data for locating the Phantom Planet isn't *complete*, on the slice. As a fail-safe, no doubt. And as you see, the slice reveals that the rest of the data was implanted in the memory of a Fse techno-worker – who was *known* to the AI, and who is still alive. Showing how recent the whole process seems to be.'

'And how unlikely,' Raishe muttered.

'So you'd need *both* the slice and the Fse,' Cade said thoughtfully, 'before you could find the Planet.'

They fell silent, then, staring in disbelief at the screen, with Cade feeling as if he had been betrayed. There can't really be an AI still existing somewhere, he thought, putting all this together. It might all be a bad joke, or a con – maybe dreamed up by the Fse tech. Though at least *he's* probably real enough . . .

'Fse' was of course short for Fsefsety, the species that formed one-third of the alien Aggregation. The Fsefsety – not a numerous species, occupying only a few worlds – were spindly insectile beings with tentacles instead of hands and feet, and gentle non-aggressive natures. They lived in tangled interweavings of family, clan and tribe, all made more complex by the way that each individual was named. For instance, the one mentioned on Cade's data-slice bore the name 'Fse-Yg', followed by a string of eleven numerals – to distinguish him from several thousand other Fse-Ygs on his home world.

And this particular Fse-Yg, wherever he was, apparently had a link with an Artificial Intelligence, which had calculated the crucial data about the Phantom Planet.

Except – there could not *be* an Artifical Intelligence.

The human worlds had spent centuries trying to perfect the science of true Artificial Intelligence – but always in vain. Time after time, the closer an AI came to equalling the miraculous capabilities of a human brain, the more *unstable* it became. And when such an AI finally slipped over the line into insanity, the results were almost always expensively destructive – and homicidal.

Finally, then, a century or so before, the technocrats had sadly abandoned the ancient dream for ever, rounded up the remaining AIs in the Human Commonwealth, and terminated them. All of them.

Or so it had always been claimed.

Cade turned bleakly away from the screen, with a question for Graklin. But he never asked it. Instead, he almost leapt out of his shoes, his nerve-ends vibrating with shock, as the terminal emitted a piercingly high-pitched shriek, like a cry of pain.

'Grak . . .!' Cade shouted, as Raishe whirled, poised for battle.

Graklin was also staring wildly around, shaking, his eyes glassy. 'The *alarm*!' he cried. 'It's a *probe*!' Gasping, he turned back to the screen, clutching the chair-arms. 'It's not possible . . . I can't believe . . . Jaxie, someone has *accessed that data*!'

8

The enemy

'Where?' Cade yelled, staring furiously around the room as if expecting to find the data-thief on a shelf.

'I've no idea,' Graklin said shakily, his hands busy at the terminal. 'I might be able to trace – oh, blast it, no, they've got a fade in the way, I can't make the link . . .'

'But you put up a privacy shield!' Raishe said suspiciously.

'I did,' Graklin said, staring helplessly at the screen. 'And there's every sort of shield and protection over *all* this room's links with the info-Net . . .' His face darkened with fury. 'How could anyone *do* this to me!'

'The hacker hacked,' Raishe murmured. 'At last the Datamaster knows what data-theft feels like . . .'

'And whoever did it,' Graklin went on, looking deeply troubled, 'must be a high-level info-tech *genius*, to break into my data-systems.'

'But it hasn't ever happened before, has it?'

Cade asked. And when Graklin shook his head, Cade's expression grew fierce. 'So unless it was a freak accident, there's someone out there who *knew* Grak would be running some special data!'

Raishe gave Graklin a suspicious look. 'How could anyone know?'

'If they knew about the data-slice,' Cade said, 'and knew I'd brought it here . . .'

'Perhaps it was the Occians,' Graklin suggested. 'They have some top-line info-experts . . .'

Cade grimaced. 'We can worry later about who did it. The point is, whoever did it now has the decoded data from the slice, and the name of the Fse who holds the rest of the data.' He paused, looking suddenly intent. 'But what he *won't* have – because it's not in this data – is information about where Fse-Yg *is.*'

'We don't have that, either,' Raishe pointed out.

'Not yet,' Cade said positively. 'But if we could find him first . . .'

'Are you going to search the galaxy for him?' Raishe asked mockingly. 'In the three days before the Starliner arrives?'

They then became aware that Graklin had brightened up a little. 'In fact,' he told them, 'we're ahead of the game. After I decoded the slice, I set my auto-systems to begin a search for Fse-Yg, and for any hint of a surviving

Artificial Intelligence. I hadn't expected quick results – especially regarding the AI.' His smile expanded. 'But you still have the luck of several devils, Jaxie. Because Fse-Yg is *here*, on Tallyra!'

'I don't *believe* this,' Raishe muttered.

But Cade merely looked overjoyed as Graklin continued. The Fse who was somehow connected with the mystery AI and the Phantom Planet had arrived on Tallyra more than a year before. At once he had spent a large sum on leasing a small single-ship, in which he had apparently gone wandering in the Deeps beyond the galactic Edge – no doubt searching for the Phantom Planet.

'But since he had only *part* of the necessary data, as the slice says,' Graklin concluded, 'he had no real chance of ever finding it, except by accident.'

'Still, he *tried*,' Cade said thoughtfully. 'So he must believe it's out there . . . Where is he now?'

'It's rather sad,' Graklin said. 'He ran out of money, couldn't go on with the search, and apparently suffered a breakdown. Now he is little more than a half-mad derelict, drunk or drugged when he can pay for the stuff, sleeping in alleys. In the Sewer.'

'Where else?' Raishe remarked.

'I've traced him,' Graklin went on, 'to a particular sleaze-bar, a seedy place where the Fse does a bit of scut-work now and then. He hangs around that area much of the time.'

'Is he carrying an AI around with him?' Raishe asked sardonically.

'Also,' Graklin added, 'I'm quite certain I wasn't bugged when that search was running. There were no alarms.'

Cade was grinning happily. 'That's brilliant, Grak. And if you can dig up anything else . . .' He paused as a thought struck him. 'Of course, we'll go shares, when we find the Planet.'

Graklin chuckled. 'Thank you, my boy. But let's not get ahead of ourselves.'

'I suppose, now,' Raishe said to Cade, 'you want to rush off to this sordid bar and find the Fse? Before this mysterious genius-hacker, who's just raided Graklin's systems, beats you to it?'

'Absolutely,' Cade said cheerfully. 'What else have we got to do in the next three days?' He grinned challengingly. 'You're not going to quit now, are you, Raishe? Aren't you a bit curious about Fse-Yg? Or are you worried about the competition?'

Her eyes flashed. 'The only thing that would *worry* me would be if someone tried to stop me getting you back to Breell. So I suppose, meanwhile, we might as well go and take a look at this Fse . . .'

'There's one thing about that bar, Jaxie,' Graklin

said gravely. 'I tried to find out who owns it, and ran into some *very* impressive info-barriers. But I did find some hints, pointing to one of the newer players in the Sewer's less legal areas. He's a strange one, named Acs – a cold fish who has made quite a reputation in a short time. You should tread carefully, my boy, when you go on to Acs's ground.'

'Don't worry,' Cade replied confidently. 'If Raishe and I can get to Fse-Yg quickly, we'll be in and out before anyone knows we're there.'

Graklin then busied himself finding them another place to stay, eventually choosing a quiet, no-questions-asked inn – not in the Sewer, but on the adjoining land mass, the rurally peaceful Sen. And when he had booked them in, through a variety of secure relays and cut-offs, Cade and Raishe drove off to find the bar where the derelict Fse-Yg might be found.

They had borrowed another city-car from among several that Graklin kept at his home. And as they set off, a soft early-summer rain was adding its murkiness to the usual mixture of smog and stinks that tended to linger over the Sewer's central basin. Yet the conditions had no effect on Cade's driving habits through the mazy streets. In fact he may have driven more impatiently than usual – out of annoy-ance at what Raishe was saying.

'You're not thinking any of this through,' she was telling him. 'You just make wild assumptions without evidence, and go charging ahead.'

'*We*,' Cade said tightly, wrenching the car around a corner into a narrow street. '*We're* charging ahead.'

She shook her head. 'No, no. I'm letting you go on with this because it's an appealing puzzle that passes the time. I may be interested, but you've completely swallowed everything. You've become convinced that the Planet is a reality – and maybe even that an AI might have survived. And you take everything Graklin says on trust. You don't *know* that what we saw on the screen actually *was* a decoding of the slice, or that the Fse is on Tallyra. Graklin just says so.'

Cade shrugged, peering at the cramped entrance to a littered lane ahead of them. 'Grak has never lied to me.'

'Cade, he's a criminal!' Raishe replied exasperatedly. 'He's built an empire on stealing and selling data! Don't you think the info about the Phantom Planet and all its riches might appeal to him?'

He glanced at her with a mocking smile. 'The way it appeals to you?'

She flushed. 'It's not the same . . .' she began defensively.

But Cade was no longer listening. Instead, he was glaring at the rear-view screen so angrily and tensely that Raishe whirled in her seat to look behind.

Two alley-bikes were behind them, with two alien figures on each, their bulging eyes fixed on the car as they closed in.

Cade swerved the car through a sliding turn into a side street. 'The city's *crawling* with Phibs!' he said furiously.

Raishe continued to look back, viper in hand now, as Cade sent the car racing into another lane before veering on to a wider road, weaving across four lanes of traffic to plunge into a cluttered alley. Yet the bikes stayed with them, unshakeable, determinedly trying to overtake.

'You'll never lose them for long,' Raishe pointed out. 'Not when they have the bio-scanners.'

'Depends on *how* I lose them,' Cade snarled, swinging the car around another turn and speeding away along a winding, pot-holed road. That led into a less busy sector of the city's central basin, where tall plain buildings loomed on either side and few people could be seen in or around them. It also seemed an unlikely place to shake off pursuers, since the streets were wide and straight, far less mazy than most of the Sewer.

'Cade . . .' Raishe began uneasily. But she broke off, firing as one of the Occian bikes surged up almost beside her window. As the riders on that bike fired, missed and dropped back, and as the other bike tried to come up on Cade's side, he gunned the car forward at top speed.

Engine screaming, the car flashed along the road – where no turn-offs could be seen at all, and where the far end of the road led into an open landscaped area like a park. Again Raishe began to protest; again she was distracted as the bikes gained on them, the riders firing.

When they came to the far end of the road, the edge of the park, they were blazing along almost in a row, a bike on either side of the car, the Occians firing wildly. Then, without warning, Cade did a wholly startling thing. He leaned towards his open window and yelled, at the top of his voice, one rasping word in the Occian language.

The aliens on the bikes seemed to stiffen, as if in shock, gaping at him. In that instant Cade stamped furiously on his brakes – so that the bikes rushed on ahead while the car skidded and fish-tailed. And it seemed for an instant, as they slid to a halt, that the car had passed through a weird flickering haze . . .

At once they were no longer looking at a road leading away through a landscaped park. Instead, they were almost at the end of a stained and rickety old wharf, with a scummy breadth of water stretching before them – with the two Occian bikes, unable to stop, making two bright splashes in its midst.

'The park's a holo-image,' Cade said with a grin in reply to Raishe's astonished look. 'This is one of the city's main rivers, where some of the waterfront companies put up the holo to hide the mess. Cheaper than fixing it up. There's a sign somewhere, but it's not easy to see – tourists often nearly go over the edge.'

Raishe stared at him. 'What was that yell you did?'

'Just about the worst insult in the Phib language,' he said with a laugh. 'I thought hearing it from me would jolt them so they wouldn't have a chance to stop.'

'And they didn't,' Raishe murmured, watching the four Occians in the river, swimming slowly towards the bank.

'Too bad you can't drown Phibs,' Cade said casually. 'Still, they won't be coming after us again too quickly.'

'So maybe it *was* the Phibs,' she said, 'who hacked into Graklin's systems.'

'Even if it was, we still need to talk to Fse-Yg,' Cade said, giving her an assessing look. 'Unless this has scared you off the idea . . .'

She glowered. 'I don't scare that easily. Let's go.'

They turned the car and drove away then, at a more sedate pace, back into the city centre. Before long, with no further alarms, they had stowed the car in a secure parking facility with armed guards, and were setting off on foot along a narrow and dirty lane. It brought them finally to some narrow and dirty stairs, which led to their goal – identified by a sign that announced 'Angels Bar'.

As they went in, Cade smiled to himself. The 'Angels' clearly referred to the group of young females, of various races and species, on view inside – wearing very little, looking not at all angelic and sitting in an oddly tense huddle. There were no visible customers, and the entry of Cade and Raishe seemed to create a nervous flutter within the group.

'Cade, I don't like this,' Raishe said, peering warily around the dim interior. 'Something's scaring these girls.'

'Maybe they think we're the law,' Cade said. 'It might help if we stop staring at them.'

They moved to one of the small round tables scattered across the bar's main area. The interior also offered some grubby sofas against the walls, a greasy syntho-wood counter at one side, and a tiny hover-stage at the far end for some form of entertainment that seemed not to be available at that time of day.

After a whispered conference among the young females, one of them rose and moved forward, wearing a patently false smile that did not disguise her tension. She was a small, shapely Illiyan, wearing only a tiny, almost transparent kilt, little more than a sash around her hips. And while she merely blinked when Cade asked for drinks, she reacted quite differently to his next request.

'I'm trying to locate a street-lag who works here sometimes,' he said easily. 'Name of Fse-Yg. Is he around?'

The Illiyan stiffened, the orange hue of her skin paling. 'What . . . what you want him for?'

'No trouble,' Cade said. 'I got a message for him, that's all. Know where he might be?'

'I . . .' She glanced around fearfully, shivering with tension. 'No. He . . . he's gone. You shouldn't be asking . . .'

She stopped, growing even more tense, her eyes widening with sudden terror. Trying to appear casual as his stomach knotted with alarm, Cade looked in the direction of her gaze.

There was a curtained door to one side of the hover-stage, at the far end of the room. And a man had stepped out through the curtains. He was not a particularly big man, but he was somehow imposing, as if he possessed some hidden, barely restrained power – like a tightly coiled spring. Lean and trim in a well-tailored tunic and trousers, he had short black hair, a narrow bony face and black eyes that were the coldest Cade had ever seen.

'Is there some difficulty, sir?' the man asked.

His voice was as icy as his eyes, totally flat and emotionless and yet holding an unmistakable threat that made Cade gather himself, while Raishe slid her hand towards her belt. Meanwhile the Illiyan was trembling with terror, staring mutely at the floor as if yearning to sink through it.

'No difficulty,' Cade replied, forcing his voice to remain calm. 'Just looking for a bit of information.'

'That commodity is not available here,' the man said frigidly.

'Are you the owner, then?' Cade asked.

'My name is Acs,' the man said, not directly answering the question. 'And I would strongly suggest to you that it is time to leave.'

Uncle Grak said he was a cold fish, Cade thought, but I've never seen colder. 'I was only asking about a Fse,' he said, making himself sound bewildered. 'What's the problem?'

'That person is no longer here,' Acs said, 'as my employee has told you.' He turned his baleful gaze on the little Illiyan. 'Although I shall be interested to find out how she came to know.'

The Illiyan made a sound like a whimper, and Cade got slowly to his feet. 'I'm more interested in where Fse-Yg went,' he said.

Acs stood motionless for a moment, his expression not changing. Then he made a small movement with one hand. At the signal, another door opened at the side of the room, next to the small counter.

Four men filed out – big, heavy, scowling men in rough clothing – and advanced into the centre of the room.

'Remove these people,' Acs ordered. 'And—' he pointed at the Illiyan – 'I will speak to you afterwards.'

The Illiyan whimpered again, wild-eyed, then joined the other females in a frantic dash through the side door by the counter.

'And remove them *convincingly*,' Acs told his men, 'so they will not be tempted to come this way again.'

One of the four men laughed, and produced a stubby, ugly rattler-gun. The other men also brought out weapons – heavy flexi-clubs or thin ice-knives – and they all moved menacingly forward.

With their first step, Cade picked up the little table to use it as both shield and weapon, while Raishe glided smoothly sideways to give herself room. But before any of them could make any further move, they were interrupted.

Through the door that led from the street came a tall, blond, broad-shouldered, cleft-chinned, remarkably handsome man – who stopped and stared open-mouthed at all the weaponry confronting him.

There was a micro-instant of motionless, startled silence. Then the thug with the rattler growled and took aim. And the room erupted into total chaos.

9

Into Hiding

The burst from the rattler missed Cade as he swung the table up in front of him. It also missed the blond man as he bounded forward, dragging a small rattler of his own from a pocket, clearly intent on trying gallantly to protect Raishe.

He discovered his mistake when he ran into Raishe's arm, like a springy bar of maxisteel, which flung him halfway across the room to get him out of the way.

And then Raishe exploded into the crimson-eyed fury of the hype.

Her enhanced speed made her a blur, a wraith, a shadow – but she was not at all insubstantial. Though she merely brushed past Cade where he crouched behind his table, the contact sent him sprawling, feeling as if he had been hit by a car. As he regained his feet, he saw Acs vanishing through the rear door – while Raishe fell upon the others.

Two of the remaining thugs howled and folded up, clutching at belly or groin, as if she had hit them both at exactly the same time. Even before they hit the floor, she hoisted the bulky man with the rattler into the air as if he was weightless, whirled him, then flung him like a squealing projectile headfirst into the counter. And while the splinters of wood and shards of glass were still flying, the storming shadow that was Raishe chopped a knife from the fourth man's grasp and back-handed him crushingly against the wall.

With no enemies left, Raishe went still, looking almost disappointed, while the crimson faded from her eyes and the manic power drained from her body. Exhaling then in a shaky breath, she sagged to one knee.

With more normal speed, Cade leaped to her side. Fumbling with the compartments of her belt, he located the velcro-sealed section that held her restorative RePlen tablets. After cramming one unceremoniously into her mouth, he heaved her awkwardly to her feet. But when her legs wavered beneath her, he stooped and with a grunt of effort hoisted her slender frame up across his shoulders.

A quick glance around showed him that the four men were either lying motionless or feebly groaning and stirring, offering no threat. And wherever Acs was, he was clearly staying well away from the violent storm that had scattered his men. So, unimpeded, Cade lurched towards the door, noting that the blond stranger – some fool of a customer, he thought, trying to be a hero – was lying stunned by the wall where Raishe had flung him, a large bump on his head.

Ignoring him as well, Cade stumbled out of the bar. Since it was in the heart of the Sewer, no one on the streets seemed even slightly curious to see a young man carrying the limp form of a woman. But nearer to the parking facility, he felt Raishe stir as the RePlen did its work. With relief he lowered her to her feet, where she leaned back against a wall, looking a bit wan but mostly restored.

In that moment, on the edge of his vision, Cade saw a sudden furtive movement – as if someone behind him had hastily dodged out of sight.

'What?' Raishe asked, aware of his sudden tension.

'Maybe nothing,' he said, looking back. 'But we might be being followed.'

'One of Acs's thugs?' she asked, looking in the same direction.

He smiled grimly. 'I can't see any of them wanting to chase us, after what you did to them.'

She nodded absently, still watching the street behind them. 'When we get into the parking place, you go on to the car. I'll wait and see who comes along.'

'Are you up to it?' Cade asked.

She gave him a look, then straightened away from the wall. 'I'm fine, though I wouldn't like to go hype again for a while. Come on. But remember – your collar's range is twenty metres. Don't go *too* far.'

They moved away towards the parking facility, where once past the doorway Cade kept on walking while Raishe slid aside into shadow. As Cade reached their car, he heard a faint shriek, a small scuffling movement – and turned to see Raishe coming towards him with one hand clamped onto the round upper arm of the micro-kilted Illiyan from the bar.

'Please,' the Illiyan babbled as they came up to Cade. 'Don't hurt me! I don't want trouble!'

'Nor do we,' Cade said, waving reassuringly at one of the guards, who was standing at the doorway staring at them. 'Why are you following us?'

'I had to get out,' she said, trembling. 'Acs would punish me . . .'

'Why?' Raishe inquired. 'Because of us?'

She tried to control her trembling. 'Because of poor Fse-Yg, I think. He's just a sad, mad street-lag, don't know his own name some days, the human girls used to tease him . . . But I guess I felt sorry for him. And Acs, even he seemed to have time for him, though Acs don't treat most folk nice at all. But then, earlier today, there's a big rush to find Fse-Yg, all sort of *secret* or something – and now the poor squit's been taken away, I don't know why. And I'm not supposed to know . . .'

'Do you know *where* he was taken?' Cade asked urgently.

She shook her head. 'I shouldn't have been watching,' she whispered. 'We were told to stay inside . . . But I had a look, and saw them pushing Fse-Yg into a robo-copter. One of those shiny ones with lights, you know, like the kind takes you to hospital . . .'

'Ambulance,' Raishe said.

'Yes,' the Illiyan went on. 'Poor thing, he was crying and howling and saying all sorts of weird stuff. I couldn't hear too well, and I didn't stay to watch. And now I got to run, because Acs knows I saw . . .' She gulped and sniffed. 'But I wanted to tell you, because maybe you could do something for Fse-Yg. He was a crazy jughead, but he was kind of sweet.'

'We'll help him if we can,' Cade told her. 'And I'm grateful to you for telling us. So . . . maybe I could help you, too.'

He reached into his pocket for what was left of his supply of cash and handed her a wad of it, at which she stared with astonished delight.

'Look after yourself,' Raishe told her.

'I'll be fine,' the Illiyan whispered. 'With this, I can get out of the Sewer for good.' She gave

105

them an anxious look. 'Which you should do, too. Because you'll have made an enemy of Acs, today. And Acs's enemies don't last long.' Her orange skin paled at the thought. 'Believe me – Acs isn't just another Sewer-shark. He's a *monster.*'

When the Illiyan had hurried away after that warning, Cade and Raishe reclaimed their car and set off again through the Sewer's tangled streets, which had grown even murkier in the evening's shadows. Cade drove silently for a while, pondering his next move, while Raishe gazed at the city or, some of the time, regarded him speculatively.

'You can be a bit surprising, at times,' she said at last. 'All that trickster charm and crooked-ness, and then you can suddenly be kind to an Illiyan girl who's nothing to you.'

Cade shrugged. 'We owed her something for trying to help us.' He grinned. 'And she was cute.'

'Every visible bit of her,' Raishe said dryly, then paused, nibbling her lip. 'By the way,' she went on in a carefully casual tone, 'what happened to the blond man who came into the bar, at the end?'

Cade glanced at her, his grin fading. 'Out cold when I saw him last. Looked like he hit his head when you sent him flying.'

Raishe frowned. 'I hope he wasn't badly hurt. I think he was trying to come to my rescue.'

'You couldn't hurt a no-brain like that by hitting him on the head,' Cade said sourly. 'Anyone who'd get in the way of a hype must have most of their lights out already.'

Raishe made no reply, seeming lost in thought, and the silence lasted all the way back to the house of Eyr Graklin, whom they visibly troubled with the tale of their encounter with Acs.

'That Illiyan gave you good advice,' the old man said. 'Acs is a very dangerous man – I think the Sewer is just starting to find out *how* dangerous. He keeps his activities well hidden, but he's known to be ruthless and very capable.'

'I'll worry about Acs later, Uncle Grak,' Cade said. 'Right now I'm thinking more about Fse-Yg. It's too much of a coincidence that he should be hustled away like that, on the same day that a hacker-thief stole the data about him from my slice.'

'Indeed,' Graklin said heavily. 'There can be no doubt, now. *Acs* must have been behind the theft. I know he has dabbled in info-tech crime, among all his ventures. And clearly he employs a *genius*-level hacker, good enough to raid my systems.'

'So now Acs will be after the Phantom Planet,' Cade said unhappily. 'And he's *ahead* of us, if he has the data from my slice and Fse-Yg too, with the rest of the data in his memory.'

Graklin nodded slowly. 'As you say. But the game may not be lost yet. They took the Fse away in an *ambulance*, didn't they? Which suggests a health facility of some sort. A private polyclinic, I imagine, equipped to deal with aliens as well as with drink and drug problems. And that may not be impossible to find.'

Raishe looked dubious. 'Surely Acs will cover his trail, especially if he has some genius hacker to help him.'

'They don't make geniuses better than Uncle Grak,' Cade said.

The old man waved a hand modestly. 'That remains to be seen. But records – especially medical records – often exist in several places at once, overlapped and duplicated in various ways. And I have years of experience of searching the datafield . . . Leave it with me. I'll call you at your new place, the inn on Sen, when I've found something. Till then, do keep your heads down and your guard up. We don't know how many *others* may be hunting you, Jax, if the rumours are spreading . . .'

Cade and Raishe left Graklin to his searches and took their leave. But, outside, Cade paused and frowned for a moment at the city-car that they had been driving.

'I think we need new transport, that no one's seen us in,' he muttered. 'And then we can go shopping, before we head for the inn where Grak has put us.'

Raishe stared. 'Shopping? Whatever for?'

'Protection,' he said briefly. 'Against Acs and anyone else who might be looking for us.'

He said no more, then, but took the mystified Raishe away in a robo-cab to one of the city's massive maxi-store complexes, near the Bridge. There they used more of Cade's cash to buy some new clothing and other slightly more surprising items. Cade also visited the info-tech department, to make another small purchase – and Raishe became mystified again when he finally went to the health-care area and picked up a container of spray-on, medicated syntho-skin.

'What's that for?' Raishe asked. 'Have you been hurt?'

Cade shook his head. 'No, and I don't intend to be. This is another sort of protection – or maybe I mean insurance.'

Then he hurried her away, with their purchases, to two privacy booths in an unattended, unoccupied rest room. But, strangely enough, no one resembling Cade or Raishe ever emerged from those booths.

10

A Knock at the Door

Two days later, Cade was staring out of a window at a serenely rural Tallyran landscape, where the lush turf and the delicate foliage of tall shrubs looked even more peaceful as evening settled upon them. But Cade felt none of that serenity, and in fact barely saw the landscape at all. He had spent nearly every moment of those two days in restless, anxious fretting, which had begun to expand into a desperation that was not too far from panic.

Because for the whole of those two days he had heard nothing at all from Graklin.

Come on, Grak, he said silently, as he had been saying over and over like a chant. *I'm nearly out of time. Two more days from now, and that Starliner will be here – and Raishe will load me on to it and take me back to jail. Unless I can find a way to talk or tempt her out of it. Come on, Grak. Call me. Come up with what I need . . .*

He had even tried calling the old man, without

Raishe's knowledge, since she would have forbidden it. After all, if the dangerous Acs did have some info-tech genius who was good enough to tap into Graklin's systems, he'd have little difficulty intercepting a Netlink call. But as Cade had grown more desperate he had ignored that risk – only to run up against a recorded message that Graklin was unavailable.

Come on, Grak, he said silently again. Only two more days . . .

Wheeling away from the window, he glanced briefly into a mirror on the wall, which showed an image that was not his usual self. Back in the maxi-store complex two days earlier, he had created a simple but effective disguise – a change of clothes, brush-in colouring to darken his hair, an ointment to darken his skin, lenses to turn his eyes brown and silica pads to fill out his cheeks and torso and make him look jowly and tubby. At the same time he had made careful use of the syntho-skin, under the padding on his torso, for a different purpose.

He had also managed to convince Raishe to change her appearance, using similar methods to turn her hair blond, darken her pale eyes and fill out her figure. In those new guises they had taken a succession of robo-cabs and copters over a meandering route, to be sure they were not followed, at last arriving in the sleepy town on the land mass called Sen to find the inn where Graklin had fixed accommodation for them. There an indifferent woman showed them to their connecting rooms – and there they had stayed, and waited, while time ticked inevitably away.

In that time, to add to Cade's troubled state of mind, Raishe had continued to be suspicious of Graklin, and of the safety of any place he had booked – even though it seemed obvious to Cade that they had to stay there to receive Graklin's all-important call. And Raishe was even more concerned about all the other dangers around them – Acs and Occians and who knew what other swarms of hijackers. So Cade was growing fearful that, before much longer, she might forget all about the Phantom Planet and its promises, and put him somewhere safe and out of action till the Starliner arrived.

Glowering into the mirror on that second evening in the inn, Cade fingered the restraint collar at his throat and thought how satisfying it might be to put something around *Raishe's* throat, and pull it tight. Still, he thought moodily, she'd just go hype and snap my spine. At that the part of his mind that held his common sense tried to point out that she had in fact saved his life, or anyway his well-being, at least twice since she had first appeared in his hotel room. But his state of mind left little room for common sense.

She's just being unreasonable, he thought unreasonably, scowling at the closed door that connected their rooms. She surely couldn't just walk away from the chance of finding the Planet. No one could turn their back on a prize like that, if there was any hope at all . . .

But still, the small voice of his common sense pointed out, that hope had become a great deal more fragile with Acs apparently ahead in the race. And now he had only two days of freedom left, with Raishe showing no sign at all of extending that deadline.

He turned his scowl towards the small Netlink terminal provided in the room, as if trying to will it to bring him a call from his great-uncle. At the same time, his stomach rumbled noisily, reminding him that it was near the time when they usually had their evening meal. They had taken all their meals in the inn, for security's sake, although the indifferent food that was on offer had done nothing for their general mood. Maybe we should risk going out, he thought. Have a nice dinner like we did in the city before, enjoy ourselves a little. It might keep her friendly . . .

He started towards the connecting door to make the suggestion to Raishe, then paused – glancing back at the Netlink, wondering whether he might try calling Graklin, first, one more time.

In that moment, there was a quiet, almost nervous knock at the door.

He turned to look at Raishe's door, but then realized. The knock had been at the other door, the one leading to the hall outside.

Nerves jumping, he gathered himself, feeling another unreasonable surge of resentment towards Raishe. I need a weapon, he thought bitterly. If I get shot now, it'll be her fault.

But then, his still vocal common sense pointed out, neither Acs nor the Phibs would be likely to bother knocking before shooting him. So, with his skin prickling under the body-padding, he went to the door and jerked it open.

In the doorway, fist raised to knock again, stood the tall, blond, too-handsome man who had come blundering into the Angels Bar.

He was wearing a fashionably bright jacket and tight calf-length leggings. He was also wearing a bump on his head, and a startled expression.

'I was . . . looking for Jaxie Cade,' the blond man said hesitantly.

'Why?' Cade asked before he could stop himself. 'I mean – *who?*'

The blond man peered at him intently. 'It's you, isn't it? You're Cade!' He nodded, still peering. 'In disguise!'

'I don't know what . . .' Cade began – but then stopped.

A slim hand had appeared above the blond man's shoulder. A hand holding a viper gun, pressing its muzzle against the man's neck.

'Let's step inside,' Raishe's steely voice said from behind the man, 'and have a little talk.'

The man froze, wide-eyed with shock, then stumbled forward into the room, helped by an impatient shove from Raishe. Cade backed up, studying the stranger, while Raishe silently closed the door before moving towards them, gun held ready.

'How did you come up behind me without making any noise?' the man asked her, sounding impressed.

'No, no,' Cade said sharply. 'That's not the question. The question is who are you, how did you get here, why are you looking for someone named Cade, things like that.'

'And what we're going to do with you,' Raishe added.

The blond man waved a hand reassuringly. 'You needn't worry. I'm not your enemy . . .'

Raishe aimed the gun between his eyes. 'You're not answering the right questions.'

'Yes, I mean, no, right, sorry,' the stranger said quickly. 'My name's Hyrd Hempel, and I'm the representative on Tallyra of the Commonwealth Intelligence Agency . . .'

'Intelligence?' Cade repeated ironically. 'I bet you didn't pass an aptitude test.'

The stranger, Hyrd Hempel, ignoring the remark, produced – slowly and carefully – the small plastic wafer that was his identification. Which Raishe studied with raised eyebrows.

'CIA,' she said musingly. 'So you're not another PReD, or any other kind of hunter.'

'Absolutely not,' Hempel said. Then realization ignited in his eyes. 'That's what *you* are, isn't it? A PReD! With the *hype*, as well as all the combat training . . .?'

'Shoot this moron, will you?' Cade muttered irritably to Raishe. 'He can't seem to grasp who's asking the questions.'

But Raishe was examining the man like a naturalist studying a new and interesting specimen. 'How did you find us?'

Hempel looked offended. 'I *am* a trained agent, you know.'

'I'd be amazed if you were *house*-trained!' Cade said angrily. 'Answer the *question*!'

'Oh . . . right.' Hempel hesitated, looking embarrassed. 'There was a bit of luck involved, I suppose. I live near here – and I was passing, two days ago, when you were arriving at this inn. Of course you were in my thoughts, after what happened when I followed you to the Angels Bar . . . So it just clicked. I knew it was you, even with the disguises.' He gazed at Raishe admiringly. 'It's the shape of your face,' he told her, 'and your legs and your . . . er . . . everything. The way you hold your head, the way you walk, like a dancer . . . I told myself, that's Raishe!' He gave her a dazzling smile. 'May I call you Raishe?'

'As long as you call her from some other planet,' Cade snarled.

Raishe's cool expression, as she inspected Hempel, did not alter. 'We're still waiting to find out what you're doing here, how you know our names, what you want with us . . .'

'Yes, of course,' Hempel said, with another splendid smile. 'It's nothing to worry about, really. In the beginning, CIA Central told me to watch you, because of all the Ph . . . the *Occian* interest in you.' His smile faded, and he went on earnestly. 'I was told you have something, Cade – some kind of object that the Phibs . . . the Occians want very badly. And there's a team of them on Tallyra looking for you. I heard that they've been watching the house of Eyr Graklin, which is where I began following you first. I nearly lost you, too, when those Occians were chasing you. It was a good trick, with the holo-image.'

'Not good enough, since you're here,' Cade muttered.

'And why *are* you here,' Raishe asked, 'rather than still just watching and following us?'

Hempel looked at her uneasily. 'Because now, some other CIA agents, higher-level, have arrived on Tallyra to speak to Cade, and maybe to negotiate to acquire the object he's got . . .'

'Without even knowing what it is?' Cade marvelled. 'Just hoping to get one up on the Phibs?'

'That doesn't explain why you're here alone, now,' Raishe insisted.

Hempel reddened slightly. 'I just thought . . . I'd make contact with you first . . .'

'So the other agents wouldn't get all the glory?' Raishe suggested, with a faint smile.

Hempel grew even redder. 'Not just that. I . . . wanted to meet you.'

Cade's snort was exasperated. 'That bump on the head must have wiped out the last of your brain cells. And all those other CIA deadwits who've landed are also wasting their time. I'm not talking to anyone about what I've got, and I'm not letting go of it. So run along and tell them that.'

Hempel looked upset. 'But I could help you . . .'

'Help?' Cade echoed. 'Like you did in the Angels Bar? The only help I could imagine getting from you would be the name of a place to eat around here.'

Hempel brightened. 'I know just the place! We could go together!'

'We are *not*,' Raishe said through her teeth, 'going to wander around outside to find some eatery, when most of the thugs and aliens on Tallyra are looking for us.'

'And anyway,' Cade added, glowering at Hempel, 'it'd have to be the best eatery on

118

the planet, to make up for the company.'

But then all three of them jumped as the Netlink terminal pinged, announcing an incoming call. Cade flung Raishe an eager, excited glance, then glowered at Hempel again.

'This is a *private* call,' he said pointedly.

'Oh, right,' Hempel said. 'I'll wait in the hall.'

Cade wanted to ask him what he was waiting *for*, but the call was far more important just then. As Hempel wandered away through the hall door, Cade hurried to the terminal, staring at the screen, with Raishe peering over his shoulder. To their surprise, it was not the call they had been expecting, from Graklin himself. It was a pre-set, automatic connection, placing a written message on the screen.

SENDING SENDING PRE-LOADED DATA-FLASH
IN SECURE MODE SENDING NOW

A micro-instant later, the terminal whispered softly and produced a strip of almost transparent tape. A data-flash, more fragile and less permanent than a silicon slice like the one Cade had taken from the Phib. But, transmitted in a single condensed pulse at the almost instantaneous speed of info-tech, a flash was extremely difficult to intercept or bug.

For a moment Cade stared at the screen that had cleared, the connection broken, before swiftly scanning the flash. Then he turned to Raishe with a frown.

'Something's gone sour . . .' he began.

But he stopped, for the hall door had begun to open, and Hyrd Hempel was peering in – with a portable mini-terminal in one hand, and a strange, troubled expression on his face.

'What do you want now?' Cade demanded impatiently.

Hempel came slowly towards them. 'I have some bad news, I'm afraid. I've just contacted my office in the city, to check in as usual, and the clerk told me . . . Cade, a known underworld character named Acs has offered a large reward for information about your location.'

'Has he, now,' Cade said darkly.

'And the Civil Patrol,' Hempel went on, 'are looking for you as well.'

'The Civs?' Cade asked, startled. 'How did they get on to me?'

'We think, at first, through someone at the Angels Bar,' Hempel said. 'But since then, there's been . . . a new development.' He gave Cade an earnestly sympathetic look. 'I'm sorry to have to tell you that, late last night, a group of Phibs tried to break into the house of your uncle, Eyr Graklin. There was a gun-fight, the Civs got involved, and . . . your uncle was shot.'

11

A Missing Fse

Cade leaped at Hempel, grabbing the man's shirt-front, almost dragging him from his feet. *'Killed?'*

'No, no,' Hempel said, pulling away, smoothing his crumpled shirt. 'He's alive – but badly hurt, and in intensive care. At a clinic that's actually not far from here . . .'

'Which one?' Cade demanded.

Hempel looked doubtful. 'You wouldn't want to go there, Cade. The Civs have it sealed off, heavily protected. It seems that Civ Central thinks there's some sort of power struggle going on among the Sewer's criminal leaders, including your uncle. The Civs don't much care which side wins, but they don't want any more fire-fights in public.'

'The Edge's priority,' Raishe commented. 'Crime is only a problem when it upsets the tourists.'

'That's right,' Hempel said. 'They don't even carry crime reports on the Netlink news-streams . . .'

'The Civs are right, though,' Cade said grimly. 'There *is* a power struggle. And we're in it.'

'And if you go to see Graklin,' Hempel pointed out, 'the Civs will grab you and hold you for questioning.'

'I know that,' Cade snarled. 'If Grak's being looked after, I'll stay away from him. Anyway, I've made contact, in a way.'

Hempel gazed at the data-flash still trailing from Cade's hand. 'Is that what that call was? Did Graklin send it?'

'None of your business,' Cade said curtly. 'In fact, it's time you went away and got on with whatever *is* your business. Preferably on another planet.'

Hempel looked injured. 'But I told you – I want to *help* you.'

Cade glowered. 'And I told you, we don't need your help. Not when you're most likely out to learn as much as you can for your bosses . . .'

'And to pick up some personal credit,' Raishe added, smiling.

'That's not it,' Hempel protested. 'At least, that's not *all* of it. I just think, with all the Phibs and criminals after you, you *need* help. And I'd like to . . .'

He halted. Raishe's faint smile had not changed, but her hand had moved with blurring speed – to level the viper-gun at Hempel's mid-riff.

'I'm sure you mean all that,' she said evenly. 'I'm also sure that if we turn down your offer and send you away, the CIA will know exactly where we are in the next thirty seconds.'

'Oh, no, Raishe, really . . .' Hempel began. But he fell silent when Raishe moved forward with the gun still levelled, backing him up – all the way back into an empty corner closet, where she closed and locked the door on his mournful expression.

Cade grimaced. 'You should've shot him.'

'We still don't know if the Phib had poison in this viper,' she said, glancing at the closet where Hempel was trying a few hopeful thumps on the door. 'It'll take him a while to break out of there. So we can get out of here, now – as we should have done before.'

'Right,' Cade agreed, waving the data-flash with a grin. 'We can go and see Fse-Yg.'

She looked startled. 'Graklin found him? Is that the message?'

'He didn't just find him,' Cade replied. 'Grak *moved* him.'

'From under Acs's nose?' Raishe asked, amazed.

Cade nodded happily. 'And despite all the data-barriers Acs set up. Grak found Fse-Yg in a private polyclinic, as he thought – and he dug out the personal code that Acs used for payment, used it to fake an order for Fse-Yg's transfer, took him away, then covered the move with shields of his own.'

Raishe's eyes were wide. 'That's very good . . .'

'He's the best,' Cade said. 'So let's go . . .'

Her expression hardened. 'With a planet full of hunters looking for you, including the CIA now, you want to go and find a down-and-out alien who probably couldn't tell you anything useful if he can talk at all?'

'*Acs* seems to think that Fse-Yg might have something to tell,' Cade reminded her.

She sniffed. 'Acs is probably crazier than you are.'

'Maybe,' Cade agreed readily. 'Maybe that's what the Phantom Planet does to people – makes them a little crazy with curiosity and hope, with the whole huge *dream* of getting rich quick, as you said before. And it's made *you* a little crazy too, Raishe, even if you won't admit it.' He smiled as she looked away with a shrug. 'So let's go have a talk with Fse-Yg, and see what he says. If we're quick and careful, there won't be any risk at all.'

'That's what you said about going to the Angels Bar,' she muttered. But when she looked at him, the gleam – of interest, and temptation – was again visible in her eyes. 'But since we've got this far – and as long as we *are* careful . . . Where would we be going, anyway? Where did Graklin put the Fse?'

Cade gave her a lopsided grin. 'Where do you think? The best place on Tallyra to hide anything. Back in the Sewer.'

At more or less the same time, in interstellar terms, on the Heart-world of the Occian Unity, the elderly Overseer in the bright green wrapping was gazing with cold and lofty concern at another, shorter Occian who wore a wrapping of dull purple.

'It is most distressing, Under-director,' the Overseer said in his toneless voice. 'The Troop-handler who preceded you in this enterprise has placed a total of thirty-three agents on the Edge-world, Tallyra. Some have been damaged – some have been arrested by the local Civil Patrol – some have even been involved in a gun-battle at the home of a known human criminal. And meanwhile the thief from Breell has eluded them all, and the object he stole has not been retrieved.'

The Under-director hissed with disapproval. 'I will assuredly do what is necessary to rectify the situation, Overseer.'

'Of course,' the Overseer replied. 'That is why you have been placed in charge. And you might also bear in mind the penalty for failure, which has now overtaken the Troop-handler.'

The Under-director's blotchy throat rippled slightly at the thought of the Dungeon of Ten Thousand Worms and the writhing toothy horrors that shared every prisoner's cell. 'Praise the Rulership in its mercy,' he mumbled.

'Praise it,' echoed the Overseer. 'Now, attend. The humans have also placed a number of agents on the planet to seek the stolen object. And there are further complications, still unclear to us, involving local criminal rivalries. With all of that, and with the uproar that your predecessor's agents have stirred on Tallyra, we can no longer concern ourselves with secrecy or subtlety. The human thief must be found, and the object wrested from him, at all speed and at any cost. To that end, the Rulership will put an *army* on Tallyra, if it must – and will eliminate any humans who impede us.'

And, also more or less at the same time, the section chief of the Human Commonwealth's Intelligence Agency, and the grey-haired woman commander, were having a frighteningly expensive person-to-person conversation – on a high-speed secure relay over the interstellar Netlines – with the leader of the CIA team that had been sent to Tallyra, who had reported some disturbing developments.

'It's not like the Phibs, acting openly on a human world,' the section chief said unhappily, peering at the team leader's face on the screen.

'They don't seem to care, sir,' the leader said. 'They're chasin' around like they've gone crazy.

126

Just last night they started a fire-fight tryin' to raid Eyr Graklin's place. Even shot a few Civs.'

The chief and his commander looked at each other. 'Maybe we need a *bigger* team there,' the commander suggested.

'I think we can handle it, ma'am,' the team leader said quickly. 'The local Civs'll co-operate with us.'

The section chief still looked worried. 'I hope so. We don't want it blowing up into some kind of *incident* . . .'

'Nevertheless,' said the commander with a decisive edge to her voice, 'it shows how much they value this thing that Jaxie Cade stole. And we mustn't forget that Cade is *human*. I don't want him harmed by Occians.'

'No, ma'am,' the team leader said, jaw jutting. 'He won't be.'

'What I mean to say,' the commander went on carefully, 'is that if Cade *has* to be harmed, or worse, to get the thing away from him, I would want it to be done to him by other humans. Specifically, by you and your team.'

Another series of robo-cabs took Cade and Raishe back into Sewr Beic, their nerves too taut with watchful tension to let them enjoy the speedsnacks that they picked up along the way. The place where Graklin had hidden the Fse turned out to be a private club, near the outskirts of the city, that offered fairly high-class gambling among other delights. And in the foyer a granite-faced guard made it clear that they were not going in to look for an alien named Fse-Yg or for any other purpose.

'You ain't members,' the guard rumbled, 'you don't get in.'

Curbing his temper, Cade summoned one of his friendly, cajoling smiles. But his persuasiveness turned out not to be needed.

'Anyhow,' the guard added stolidly, 'that Fse yer talkin' about, he ain't here no more.'

Cade's mouth fell open. 'He's *gone*? Where?'

'Dunno,' the guard said. 'Dunno why he was here inna first place. I don't get told stuff like that.'

'Did you see him go?' Raishe asked.

'Nope.' The guard's stony face was softened by a slightly envious grin. 'He musta been happy, though, when he went. I heard he won a bundle on 3-D roulette, upstairs, earlier.'

Cade turned blankly away. So it ends here, he thought numbly. With Grak out of action, there's no hope of finding Fse-Yg again, in just two days. And that means there's nothing to offer Raishe, to tempt her out of taking me back . . .

'Do you think Acs has got him again?' Raishe asked.

'I suppose,' Cade said miserably. 'It looks like he's even quicker and smarter than we thought.'

She nodded, with a tinge of sympathy and perhaps also disappointment in her eyes. 'That's it, then . . .' she began.

But she and Cade were both silenced when the club's door swung open – and Hyrd Hempel strode in towards them, smiling brightly, looking delighted with himself.

'How . . .' Raishe said, then caught herself as she realized. 'Did you put a tracer bug on us?'

Hempel's smile grew even brighter. 'On my way out of your room when that call came in. What did you expect?'

'I said you should've shot him,' Cade grumbled.

'No hard feelings, though,' Hempel went on warmly, to Raishe. 'I can understand why you did what you did. And I want you to know that I haven't reported any of this, yet. Because I still want to help you.'

But if Cade or Raishe had an answer to that offer, it was never voiced. At that moment the door crashed open again, and a squad of blue-uniformed Civil Patrolmen charged into the foyer, waving stun-clubs and rattler-guns.

12

Too Many Pursuers

By instinct, forgetting about the collar, Cade turned and ran towards a door at the rear of the foyer. Also by instinct, with armed men advancing and her prisoner escaping, Raishe ran as well, only a half-step behind Cade. Hempel was at their heels, clearly determined not to be left behind again.

They heard a chorus of angry shouts as the Civs galloped in pursuit, and a rattler hummed as one of them fired. But the shot missed as the three of them slammed through the door and sprinted away along a corridor. Swinging around a corner, out of sight of the Civs, they burst through some double doors into a broad, unoccupied lounge. Tall glass doors on the far side opened on to a paved patio – with the shadowy foliage of a garden visible beyond it.

Hurtling across the lounge, they found the glass doors locked. But Raishe's foot slammed against the lock with explosive power, blasting the doors open. Dashing out on to the darkened patio, aware that the pursuing Civs had still not reached the lounge, Cade looked frantically around for the best way out of the garden.

But instead, they froze – when several beams of white light flared out of the darkness, transfixing them.

And from the leafy shadows stepped another troop of armed Civs, who had had the sense to cover the club's back door.

Sickened and furious, Cade stayed still and raised his hands, with Raishe and Hempel following suit. Then the pursuing group of Civs came panting up and milled around with the others, all laughing and congratulating one another as the three prisoners were offhandedly searched for weapons, handcuffed and hauled away to the pair of patrol-vans waiting outside the club. Cade and Raishe stayed silent during that time, perhaps because Hempel's loud protests – along with the discovery of his small rattler-gun in his pocket – earned him a brutal jab in the belly from a stun-club, which folded him up into a groaning heap.

The Civs' merry self-congratulation continued as one group heaved Cade and his companions into the back of a van and set off, with the rest of the Civs following in the second vehicle. Cade paid little attention to them, more concerned with looking for possibilities of escape – mostly centred on Raishe and her powers in the hype. But she showed no sign of doing anything aside from glaring at Cade, clearly blaming him for their predicament.

If I could find a way to *hit* her, Cade thought morosely, it might set off the hype. At least it might stop her giving me dirty looks. It was probably Hempel's fault, anyway, that the Civs caught up with us . . .

But in that he was wrong, as he learned when his attention was caught by the talk among the Civs in the van.

'What I'd really like to know,' one of them said, 'is who it was called us to say where we could find these three.'

'Maybe a law-abidin' citizen,' another said, 'doin' his civic duty.'

It was obviously a standard joke among Civs in the Sewer, and produced loud ironic laughter. 'Whoever it was,' a third Civ pointed out, 'they said these three were involved in some kind of raid on a sleaze-bar, the Angels. So I bet it was somebody there – maybe the owner.'

That led the Civs into leering comparisons of the girls in the Angels Bar and those in similar places. So Cade went back to thinking about escape, and to scowling at Raishe. *Do* something, Cade told her silently. Get us out of this . . . He studied the smooth curve where her leggings were drawn tight over her thigh. I might just be close enough to kick her, to start the hype, he thought. But hype or no hype, I'd really *like* to kick her . . .

But in that moment the van rumbled to a halt, the doors were opened, and the Civs led the prisoners into a small stark building that was the local Civil Patrol post. There, Cade, Raishe and the stunned Hempel were searched again, a little more thoroughly. The Civs seemed to doubt the genuineness of Hempel's and Raishe's IDs, and were greatly amused by Cade's and Raishe's body-padding and the rest of their disguises. That seemed to offer further evidence of their guilt, and it was then all briskly removed, although the Civs failed to spot the syntho-skin on Cade's bare torso, or to recognize his restraint collar for what it was.

At last, with routine blood samples and retina photographs taken, the three prisoners were led away to separate cells, without a chance for Cade and Raishe to do more than glare at each other once more in mutually helpless anger. Their cells must have been within twenty metres of one another, since Cade's collar remained inactive. And so did everything else, from then on, aside from the relentless passage of time.

As the hours crept by, Cade sat in misery and stared at nothing much at all, seeing only that his dreams about the Phantom Planet were lying in ruins around him. Or, at other times, thinking about his injured great-uncle, about a missing Fse and an unlikely Artificial Intelligence, about the menace of the Phibs and of Acs. And also about Acs's unknown genius-hacker, who must somehow have found Fse-Yg's new hiding place and set the Civs to watching it . . .

Despite all those torments, as the night wore on, he dropped wearily into an uneasy doze – to awaken in daylight when a surly Civ arrived with a fabri-tray of food and a curt refusal to answer any questions. So the day began to inch forward as the night had done. Probably, Cade came to think, the Civs were investigating and cross-checking and finding more things to charge them with. I wonder, he thought dolefully, if they'll send me back to Breell or put me away here on Tallyra. And if they'll let Raishe go, to catch that Starliner by herself tomorrow . . .

Oddly, he found that idea troubling as well – the idea of Raishe leaving the Edge, of his never seeing her again. Forget it, he told himself bitterly. If you ever *did* see her again, she'd probably just drag you off to jail to complete her contract . . .

He was still lost in his unhappy thoughts and imaginings, later in the day, when a squad of Civs stamped into the cell and dragged him away, out of the building, to where he saw Raishe – apparently no longer in custody, and wearing her belt again – standing next to a shaky-looking Hempel, and arguing fiercely with a red-faced Civ captain.

'You *can't* hold Cade!' she was saying, her pale eyes ablaze. 'You've verified my ID – and he's an escaped convict and my prisoner, which takes precedence!'

'Save it, lady,' growled the captain. 'You should be glad we ain't chargin' you with somethin'. Anyway, Central HQ is takin' over the whole mess, an' they're welcome to it. They want to ask you all some questions, so go argue with them.' He gestured to his men. 'Get 'em outa here.'

Again they were loaded into a van, which sped away through the city. Around them the Civs chatted merrily, from which Cade discovered that he was suspected of many crimes including assault, resisting arrest and perhaps spying for the Occians. But he kept silent, as before – although Hempel was protesting again, and being ignored again, while Raishe merely sat and glared furiously at everyone.

Without warning, something slammed into the side of the van with a thunderous, crunching, battering impact.

All of them, Civs and prisoners, were hurled painfully around in a flailing tumble as the van toppled over on its side and skidded along the street before crashing into a building. So all of them were lying in a semi-dazed heap when the doors of the van were wrenched open.

Outside, the street was aswarm with Phibs.

*   *   *

Nearly two dozen grey-wrapped aliens, as far as Cade's dazed mind could count them, were surrounding the wrecked van, viper-guns ready. Otherwise the street was empty, since any nearby people had sensibly got out of the way at the first sign of trouble. Swiftly the Occians pulled Cade out of the wrecked van and dragged him towards a heavy, blunt-nosed magnitruck which had been used to ram the Civ vehicle.

'Where is it, human filth?' spat one of the aliens, whose wrapping bore the insignia of higher rank, and who spoke the human tongue fairly clearly. 'Where is the object that you stole?'

Cade ignored him, glancing around, weighing up his chances of making a run for it – before remembering that Raishe was still in the Civ van, so that the collar would drop him twenty metres away, even if the Phibs did not.

A hard webbed hand slammed bruisingly against his head. 'Tell where it is,' another Occian hissed, 'or you die!'

The leader with the insignia intervened with a hiss. 'He knows we cannot kill him until we have the object . . . Bring the others – the thief's companions who are also prisoners. We will torment *them*, to make him speak.'

Taut with tension, Cade watched Raishe being dragged from the Civ van, looking half-stunned, along with the limp form of Hempel who seemed again to have hit his head. The three of them were hurried into the magnitruck, and as it roared away on its outsized wheels Raishe stirred, peering around the windowless interior at their Occian captors.

'What's going on?' she asked blankly.

Cade gave her a bleak look. 'Our alien brethren seem to have caught up with us.'

The Occian leader bared serrated teeth. 'With our bio-scanners, which human technology cannot hope to duplicate, it has been effortless to track you, vermin. Especially when you were fool enough to return to this dung-heap.'

'But you're in trouble now, aren't you?' Cade snarled. 'The Civs won't take kindly to what you've just done.'

'An inept force on a corrupt world,' the Occian said dismissively. 'They will not find us before we have achieved our goal and reclaimed the object that is rightfully ours.'

With that the leader turned away, pointedly joining his troop in a graphic discussion of the best ways to force Cade to give up the slice. So Cade leaned back against the side of the magnitruck, knowing that the alien was probably right about the chances of the Civs finding them. The Occians would have some kind of hideout – maybe beyond the city outskirts. And when they reached that hideout, he knew, things would get a *lot* nastier . . .

After an almost unbearable time, and more desperate but vain attempts to think of a way out, he heard a change in the sound of the truck's huge wheels. It suggested that they were rolling along a more uneven surface – like a country road. Out of the city, as he had thought. He grew even more tense and frantic, wondering how there could be the tiniest hope of escape out there in the open, away from the Sewer's labyrinth that he knew so well. And he was cold with dread, a trickle of icy sweat running down his back, when the truck finally rolled to a stop.

Outside, surprisingly, twilight had begun to spread its shadows, made darker by a heavy over-cast. As they all emerged from the magnitruck, Cade could see that they were indeed out of the city – on a bare patch of land surrounded by straggles of brush. At one side stood a low blocky building like some sort of stor-age facility, clearly the Occian hideout, since the aliens began to herd Cade and Raishe to-wards it, dragging along the still half-unconscious Hempel.

But they were still only a few steps from the truck when Cade glimpsed a small cylindrical object arcing through the air towards them.

In the next moment, with an enormous deafen-ing blast, a wave of force like a mighty invisible hammer struck at them, flinging their stunned bodies to the ground.

*   *   *

Cade was dimly aware of voices and dark shapes around him, vaguely felt hands gripping him. But then he realized that they were *human* shapes and voices and hands, and that jerked him back to full consciousness.

'Chuck the lizards into the building,' a hard commanding voice was saying, 'an' make sure you get all their guns. Then burn the lock, so they won't get out in a hurry.'

Cade peered at the shadowy human shapes, wondering if the blast – a concussion grenade, he guessed – had been a Civ counter-attack. But in the next moment he realized the truth, with something less than delight. The human new-comers were wearing plain tunics and trousers, not uniforms, and holding pyro-guns, not rattlers. And one of them was staring down at a limp form that had been lying half-hidden by unconscious Occians.

'What d'you know!' that man cried. 'It's Hand-some Hyrd!'

Wonderful, Cade thought dispiritedly. The CIA.

The hands that had pulled him to his feet were still keeping a tight grip on him, which he tried to shake off. 'Thanks,' he muttered. 'You can let go now.'

'I don't think so,' said the hard-voiced leader, stepping towards him. 'We're gonna take you somewhere quiet, where you're gonna answer some questions – about what you've got that the Phibs want so bad, an' what you've done with it.'

Am I, Cade said to himself, seeing that Raishe was also on her feet, awake but swaying a little, also firmly held. He also noted that it was growing even darker, while most of the CIA men were busy dragging fallen Occians into the storehouse. If Raishe and I broke free at the same time, Cade thought, we might make it to the bushes at the edge of the field. He began to stare intently at Raishe, to try to signal her somehow, to get the idea across.

But in that moment, from the very patch of brush he had in mind, the scorching blast of a pyro-gun burst out – freezing the CIA men in shock as it painted a red line of fiery warning across the darkness.

It was followed by a voice from the same dark patch of brush. 'Drop all your guns. Now. Or we start burning legs.'

Reluctantly, the CIA men threw their guns down, glaring with helpless fury into the darkness that hid the speaker.

'Cade,' the unseen speaker went on from the brush, 'you and the lady come on over here.'

Cade hesitated for an instant, gathering himself, seeing that Raishe was doing the same. But their chance did not come.

'Cade,' the voice from the darkness said, 'don't try anything. You wouldn't make it. Just come *on*.'

I bet I can guess who's got us *now*, Cade thought unhappily as he and Raishe moved away towards the darkened brush. And there he became more certain, when they were roughly seized by tall, bulky figures and bundled into a long dark limocopter, which lifted almost soundlessly from the ground and whirled them back towards the city.

There were half a dozen men in the limo, big and tough-looking. Just like the heavies from the Angels Bar, Cade thought. Sent by Acs.

'Thanks for the rescue,' he said sardonically. 'Did you just happen to be passing?'

One of the men gave a small mirthless laugh. 'We saw the Phibs grab you in the city, but we couldn't land there. So we followed them – right behind the CIA. No trouble at all.'

'Who *are* you?' Raishe demanded. 'Where are you taking us?'

'You'll see soon enough,' the man said shortly.

And he said no more, so that eventually Cade and Raishe were silenced as well, merely staring blankly out of the window at the dark empty sky.

At last, after a ride that seemed endless, the limo drifted down to the ground, next to a darkened, flattish, oddly curved building on a stretch of wasteground in an outer section of the city.

Still wordless, the men took Cade and Raishe into the building, along a lengthy, narrow passageway and into a sizeable room comfortably furnished with chairs and sofas like a lounge. There they halted – and Cade, with a sudden sense of danger, spun around to face his captors.

The man nearest him smiled. 'This is it. End of the road.'

And his hand began to move, bringing up his gun.

As ever, Cade reacted from pure instinct. Lunging forward, he slammed the man aside with a shoulder and ran. He was at the door before anyone else began to move and then, driven by near-panic, he sprinted away along the corridor that seemed to stretch endlessly before him.

He almost made it.

The outer door was only half a dozen strides away, the pursuing men had only just entered the corridor at the other end. But – although he heard no shot – he was halted as if he had run into a wall.

A wall of soft but unyielding darkness that stopped him and engulfed him and switched him off.

13

Above the Clouds

He could hear his name being spoken, sounding very far away, dragging him out of a cosy dream that melted as he clutched at its fragments. Groaning silently, he gave in, letting himself rise towards the brightness.

'Jaxie?'

His eyes opened, focusing with difficulty. He was lying on a couch looking up at a concerned expression on the face of Eyr Graklin – who was supposed to be half-dead after a gun-fight . . . And there was Raishe, too, bending over Cade's supine form. And behind her, a bulky man with a gun in his hand . . .

As Cade sat up swiftly, fighting a sweep of dizziness, the gunman gave him an apologetic smile before putting the weapon away under his coat – which is what he had been starting to do, before Cade had run. Then Cade realized that they were all back in the comfortable lounge at the end of the corridor.

'Uncle Grak?' he croaked. 'What *is* this?'

Graklin also looked apologetic. 'I'm sorry about the guns and the mystery, Jax. These are my people. I told them to bring you here without fail, and without revealing where you were being taken, or by whom.'

'They take you literally, don't they,' Raishe said dryly. 'But at least Cade now knows exactly how the collar works.'

Cade blinked, realizing at last what it was that had felled him. His run had taken him more than twenty metres from Raishe . . . And that would be the antidote to the collar's narcotic, he thought, watching Raishe tuck a small spray-syringe back into her belt.

He shook his head dazedly, turning to Graklin again, seeing that the old man looked tired and drawn but otherwise entirely healthy. 'Are you all right, Grak?' Cade asked. 'I thought you were in intensive care . . .'

'I'm sorry,' Graklin said again. 'I let it be known that my gunshot wound was more serious than it is, so people would think I was out of action. In fact it was only a graze. I'm in no danger.'

'I wish I could say the same,' Cade replied, glowering in the direction of Graklin's men who were silently filing out of the room. 'We've had a lot of fun, being captured and threatened by Civs and Phibs and the CIA, all taking turns.'

Graklin nodded sympathetically. 'I know it's

been unpleasant for you. That's why I had you brought here, Jaxie. For your safety.'

'Where *is* here?' Raishe asked. 'And why should this Sewer rat-hole be safer than any other?'

Graklin began to reply, then paused. In that moment a powerful but muffled rumbling could be heard all around them, and the floor beneath them began to vibrate slightly. At once Cade struggled uneasily to his feet, while Raishe stared tensely around, poised for action.

But Graklin raised a reassuring hand. 'Calm yourself,' he said. 'This is in fact my private strato-barge, and we are just lifting off. To spend a while in the air, above all the violence and peril of the city. I've had all your things collected up and brought here.'

He gestured towards a cabinet at the far end of the lounge, where Cade and Raishe found their bags and all their possessions. But Raishe's face clouded with anger when she saw the crack across the screen of her portable Netlink, and found that it was no longer working.

Graklin looked appalled. 'I can't think how that happened,' he said apologetically. 'I'll have it repaired or replaced, of course.'

She scowled at him. 'How soon? I need to call the spaceport to confirm the Starliner's arrival time.'

'Do you imagine I have no terminals here?'

Graklin said, smiling. And, beckoning, he floated away in his servo-chair, out of the lounge to an adjoining room that was a compact version of the info-tech sanctum in his home. There, on an impressively multifunctional Netlink terminal, Raishe called the spaceport and made her inquiry – to a disdainful robo-voice, with the spaceport data-board displayed on the screen.

'The next Starliner arrival at Tallyra,' the robo-voice intoned, 'has been delayed for a further forty-eight hours, due to a malfunction in the life-support back-up system.'

Raishe snapped the terminal off, pale with fury. 'Two more *days*?' she cried. 'This is *grotesque*! I feel as if I've been *jinxed*!'

'I don't,' Cade said, grinning happily.

'Still, it might have been worse,' Graklin said to Raishe comfortingly. 'And we can stay aloft for that time, in safety, if you like.'

She turned her angry glare towards him, hesitated, bit her lip, then nodded stiffly. 'All right. As long as we get to the spaceport without any problems when it's time.'

'Of course, of course,' Graklin agreed. 'But for now, I'm sure you'd like to make yourselves comfortable, perhaps change and freshen up. And later, you might tell me in more detail what's been happening . . .'

He touched a button on the servo-chair, which

brought one of the silent men to show Cade and Raishe to two small adjoining bedrooms. After long and much-appreciated showers and changes of clothes, they returned to the lounge. Where Graklin was waiting with an array of food and drink, and where he urged Cade to recount their recent adventures.

The story – and especially the new disappearance of Fse-Yg, from the club where Graklin had hidden him – left the old man deeply troubled. 'Most disturbing,' he mused, 'and most odd. Of course it must be Acs who has Fse-Yg again – after penetrating more layers of my info-security, as before. I wouldn't have thought it *possible* . . . And I don't imagine it would be so easy to find Fse-Yg again, since Acs will cover his tracks far more thoroughly this time.'

'But we won't be *looking* for the Fse,' Raishe said sharply. 'We're staying up here for the next forty-eight hours, aren't we? And then Cade will be on his way back to Breell, and he can *forget* about the Fse, the mythical AI, the Phantom Planet and everything.'

'I'm not likely to forget,' Cade muttered gloomily.

'Nor am I, I must say,' Graklin agreed, looking slightly abashed. 'I seem to have become quite fascinated by all these mysteries.'

'I bet you have,' Raishe murmured.

'In fact,' the old man went on, ignoring her sarcasm, 'I've been going on with the data-searches this past while. As you might expect, my auto-systems have still found no trace anywhere of a surviving Artifical Intelligence. But I also set up a separate search to back-track Fse-Yg, to see where he had been before coming to Tallyra. And I've had a third search running at the same time, similarly back-tracking the Occian thief who had the slice on Breell.'

'That couldn't have been easy,' Cade commented.

'It wasn't,' Graklin said. 'Occians keep very low profiles when they visit human worlds. And it all seems sadly inconclusive . . . The Occian landed on several planets before reaching Breell – but none of them seems to show a record of a small data-slice being stolen. And Fse-Yg in his own travels has left a tangled trail which has been blurred by disruption – perhaps accidental, perhaps not – in the data-stores on a few worlds. But my searches did pry out one interesting little link.'

'What?' Cade asked curiously, as Graklin paused and reached down to the tiny screen on his chair's control panel.

'Yes,' the old man went on, as a line of data on the screen refreshed his memory. 'That was it. One of the worlds visited by the Occian thief was a remote and rather backward place named

Lannamur. Which is *also* the name of a planet where Fse-Yg seems to have lived awhile.'

As Cade leaped to his feet, fizzing with excitement, Raishe sniffed. 'You said it's a backward world,' she pointed out. 'Not a likely place to find a valuable data-slice.'

Graklin smiled. 'But it is. Lannamur has two moons, now transformed into space stations and mini-colonies. The planet may be backward, but the moons have a reputation for high-tech research and development.'

'Terrific!' Cade cried. 'That *has* to be the place where the Phib stole the slice!'

'So what,' Raishe said wearily. 'The slice isn't there now, the Fse isn't there . . .' She gave Graklin a withering look. 'And I don't suppose you found an operational AI there.'

'No,' Graklin replied. 'I fear not.'

'There you are,' Raishe went on. 'As I said, Cade, you can *forget* this crazy dream. Since Acs also has the data from the slice, and probably now has Fse-Yg again as well, he has everything he needs to find the Phantom Planet. If it exists, Acs will have grabbed it before you get out of prison.' She held up a hand as Cade tried to interrupt. 'And there is *nothing* now, I promise you, that could keep me from delivering you back to that prison.'

Graklin sighed, nodding sadly. 'I fear that Raishe is right, Jaxie. Acs is holding all the cards, while you have only the original data-slice.' He paused, peering at Cade. 'You do still have it, don't you?'

Cade saw Raishe give him a dubious glance. And although he still did not share her distrust of Graklin, some instinct made him cautious. 'The slice is safe,' he said vaguely.

'I'm glad,' Graklin said. 'Although I'm not sure that *you* are safe, my boy. While you have the slice, Acs might still feel that you pose some threat to his hope of finding the Planet. And the Occians, the CIA and others may still pursue you for it. Even if . . . *when* Raishe puts you away in prison, you could remain at risk.'

'What do you suggest, then?' Cade asked gloomily.

The old man shrugged. 'It can be good business practice to cut your losses when things look threatening . . . You might consider *selling* the slice, Jaxie. To the highest bidder. It should bring a substantial price, and you would be alive afterwards to enjoy it.' He glanced at Raishe. 'When you come out of prison, of course.'

Cade shook his head slowly. 'I don't know, Grak. After what I've been through to get the slice and keep it, I'm in no rush to give it up . . .'

'How could you sell it, anyway?' Raishe wanted to know. 'It's useless without Fse-Yg . . . And the Phibs and the CIA and who knows who else would still go after a new owner . . .'

'A buyer wouldn't need to know that, beforehand,' Cade said vaguely.

Raishe's mouth tightened. 'Of course. I was foolish enough to imagine it would be an *honest* sale.'

'Or,' Graklin put in, 'you might find a buyer who was willing to accept all those difficulties.'

'Like who?' Raishe asked suspiciously. 'You, perhaps? Is that what this is about, Graklin? Are you after the Phantom Planet for yourself?'

Graklin raised his eyebrows. 'Why, no. I'm simply concerned for Jaxie's safety.'

'And I've already said that Grak would share in whatever I get,' Cade told Raishe, frowning.

'Maybe he's not happy with just a share,' Raishe retorted. 'Maybe he wants all of it. Maybe *that's* why he had us brought here – to get the slice away from you. Remember, Cade, we're stuck on this barge. We can't leave until Graklin lets us. *If* he lets us.'

'Raishe . . . !' Graklin said, looking injured. 'If you and Jaxie were to leave, you might soon be under threat again from all your enemies. But you're certainly *free* to go, whenever you wish.'

Raishe studied him doubtfully. 'The only way I can know that for sure is if you land again and open the door. Preferably at the spaceport.'

'Will you lighten up?' Cade asked her irritatbly. 'I'd just as soon not go back to playing pass-the-prisoners with the Phibs and the CIA and everyone. Grak isn't the enemy, Raishe. Believe me.'

She seemed about to continue the argument, looking unconvinced, but then shrugged and turned away. In the awkward silence that followed, Cade wandered idly over to a window-port, staring thoughtfully out at the thick cloud layer that lay below the cruising stratobarge.

'You know,' he said after a moment, 'it's really not a bad idea – to offer the slice for sale.'

Raishe stared at him. 'That's a quick about-turn.'

'I didn't say *sell* it,' Cade replied. 'I said *offer* it. Specifically, to Acs.'

'You've lost your mind,' Raishe snapped.

He smiled. 'I don't plan to go near Acs if I can help it. I just want to get him *talking*. Let him get smug and confident, thinking I've given up, so that he might lower his guard and let something slip about where he's hidden Fse-Yg.'

'There's no *point* . . .' Raishe began, glaring.

But Graklin intervened with a chuckle. 'I could try to contact Acs on the Netlink,' he said, 'if you really want to play this game.'

'That's all it is – a game,' Raishe insisted. 'Even

if Acs told you outright where Fse-Yg is, wha
do you think you could do? Fly down and visit
him?'

'We might think of something,' Cade said with
a cheerful smile. 'At least it would pass the time
during the next forty-eight hours.'

'That's how you got me into this mess in the
first place,' Raishe said through her teeth.

But she trailed along, taut with disapproval,
as Cade followed the old Datamaster back again
to the barge's version of his sanctum and the
multi-functional terminal. At once Graklin went
to work, his hands plunging deep into the terminal's extensors to glide expertly among the
polyfaces and cryptoforms, while also murmuring
into the voice-activated function. Time passed,
Cade fidgeted and Raishe watched suspiciously.
But before long, Graklin leaned back with a
disappointed sigh.

'So many dead ends,' he murmured. 'Someone
is uncannily skilled at camouflaging Acs, screen-
ing his location.'

'You'll get him,' Cade said reassuringly. 'Try
again later.'

Graklin dispiritedly drew his hands away from
the Netlink. But as the screen began to clear,
all three of them tensed with sudden surprise
– when a soft chime sounded within the link,
announcing an incoming call.

on the screen appeared the cold, bony, expressionless face of Acs.

'Myr Graklin,' Acs said, his voice as empty as his expression. 'I am informed that you are making efforts to locate me. You need trouble yourself no further. I have four fully armed skyfighters surrounding your barge – and I strongly advise you to offer no resistance.'

14

Chamber of Horrors

Cade leaped frantically to a window-port, cold with shock as he stared out at the flat, ominous shape of one of the skyfighter ships keeping pace with the barge.

Whirling, he stared at Graklin. 'Can you get away?'

'The barge couldn't outrun a fighter, Jax,' Graklin said shakily. 'Or outshoot it. They could destroy us in a moment.'

So Cade could only turn back to stare out of the port again, desperate but helpless, as the gunships herded the barge down through the clouds. They were heading towards a point speci-fied by Acs – a high plateau deep in the heart of the mountains that rose at the far end of the land mass, Wen. There the skyfighters hovered menacingly while the barge lowered itself onto a pad near a complex of stark ceramistone build-ings, looking like extensions of the rocky crags around the plateau. A rec-centre, Cade guessed – and a very new one, with some parts still under construction, and all of it entirely deserted.

Once the barge was down, the fighters landed at speed. A troop of armed men poured from them, bringing everyone off the barge at gunpoint. Graklin's handful of men were taken away towards one of the side buildings – but Cade, Raishe and Graklin were herded into the central area of the complex. After trudging through empty corridors and bare rooms where the plastiwalls were still fresh, their guards pushed them finally through a heavy door into a long, wide chamber with tall windows along one side and at one end and skylights in the ceiling. And that central area of the chamber was not at all bare and empty, but was furnished – almost overcrowded – in an unexpected and dreadful way.

It's like a stage set, Cade thought, his skin crawling. Or a museum, or exhibition . . .

But if so, it was an exhibition of horror.

The display in that sunken area contained nothing but instruments and devices of *torture*. They seemed mostly to come from the darker regions of ancient history on humanity's first home, Old Earth. Cade recognized the flat metal framework with a fire-bed underneath, where victims could be literally grilled, and two wooden racks with ropes designed for stretching and tearing. He saw plenty of smaller devices for twisting or crushing or slow impaling; he saw chains and ropes and wires, vats of foul water or searing acid, a huge variety of whips and scourges, saws and axes, hooks and prods, shears and tongs . . . And he also spotted more up-to-date items in that vile assembly of torment, including one of the Illiyan jungle creepers whose seeds germinate in flesh, rooting in a victim's body – along with some of the tiny Occian blood-worms who also burrow into flesh to feed and grow in the arteries until the victim dies.

Some of the older devices were simulations – plastic ropes treated to look like old hemp, syntho-wood frames made to look crude and splintery, maxisteel covered with false stains and rust – but Cade had no doubt that most of the exhibits, if not all, were in full working order.

Acs is just trying to scare us, he told himself, as he and the others were urged down into the central area. It's some kind of psych-trick . . . But then, as he and the other two prisoners were halted, he knew at once what was going to happen.

The armed guards had fixed filter-masks over the lower part of their faces. And before Cade or Raishe could begin to react, one of the men raised a bulb-like object, and a cloud of narco-gas hissed out to wrap them in darkness.

Cade woke with a dry mouth and a tightness in his head, as if his skull had shrunk. But both those sensations faded by comparison with the far worse realization that he could not move a muscle from the neck down. Cold with fright, he wondered whether the gas had been a paralytic, and whether its effects were permanent . . . But then he strained his neck to peer down at himself, and almost gasped aloud with relief. He wasn't paralysed, and it wasn't permanent. He was simply, but unusually, tied up.

The bonds were as thick as heavy cables, as smooth as new plastic. Glistening unpleasantly, they were like the coils of huge improbable serpents, wrapped around Cade's torso to bind his arms to his sides, and around his legs from the knees down. Soligel, he thought, his heart sinking. Which can't be broken or stretched or shifted in any way once it's set. Though, he reminded himself, it *can* be melted by some acids, and cut by an unusually sharp blade . . .

Straining his neck again, he saw that he was lying on the narrow wooden platform of one of the racks. But he was not actually tied to the device, so it seemed that his limbs were not immediately due to be stretched and dislocated. Nearby, he saw Raishe – eyes closed, unmoving – lying bent backwards over a metal stretching-wheel, her wrists and ankles fastened with chains that also appeared to be soligel disguised as metal. And on Cade's other side Graklin sat slumped and unconscious, wrists bound by more soligel, in his servo-chair – which had been immobilized, its control mechanisms lying shattered on the floor, beyond repair.

The psych-trick goes on, Cade thought grimly. He saw that they were alone in the room, with no sign of their captors, showing how confident the enemy was in their helplessness. Don't let it get to you, he ordered himself. Wait and see, wait for a chance . . . Just wait.

Acs did not keep him waiting long.

He came into the room swiftly and silently, followed by four of his men who took watchful positions by the door, heavy pyro-rifles in their hands. And Acs clearly had not come to mock, or gloat, or threaten – but simply to make it clear what he wanted, and how he was going to get it.

He examined Cade silently for a moment, his eyes as cold and pitiless as winter rain, his bony face without expression. Then he glanced over at Graklin as the old man regained consciousness, peering and blinking, slowly grasping the facts of their captivity. With a glance at Raishe, who was still motionless with closed eyes, Acs turned his gaze back to Cade.

'I want you to listen carefully,' he said in his bleak voice, 'so you will have no illusions about your situation.'

'I'm fresh out of illusions,' Cade muttered.

Acs paused as if considering the remark, then continued. 'First, this recreation complex belongs to me and is not yet open to the public. This chamber, when operational, will offer an authentic display of the ancient human practices of torture. Customers may watch or participate, using mannequins or volunteering to be victims, as they wish. The essential fact is that all the devices *work*, despite their antique crudity. I have no impulses to sadism, Cade, but I know that many humans have, and I expect the exhibit to be a popular attraction. More importantly, at this time, you must understand that I will not hesitate to use the devices if it is necessary. And you must harbour *no* unrealistic hopes of escape or rescue.'

He paused, watching, while those dire points sank in.

'Now,' he went on, 'regarding the data-slice that you acquired on the planet Breell . . . It was unintentionally useful of you to bring it here, to Tallyra. I know that the Occian who first stole it did not have it copied – and that, therefore, no copies of it exist elsewhere on any other planets.'

'Don't be too sure,' Cade snarled.

Acs's expression did not change. 'In fact I am sure. There would have been no logical point in *your* taking hard copies of the slice – and no copies were discovered in a thorough search of every place where you and the woman have been on Tallyra, and of Eyr Graklin's home and vehicles. As for the possibility of copies held in Graklin's data-systems, I have devised a short-term, single-function virus that I have inserted into those systems – and through them into the entire data-field of Tallyra. The virus will seek and erase *only* the data from that one slice. At this moment, then, it is almost a complete certainty that that data exists *only* on the single, original slice, and on the hard copy that I took of it from Graklin's systems.'

He paused, studying them, but neither of them responded. Graklin was looking appalled by the announcement of such a focused, specific virus, which showed the frighteningly high level of info-tech skill that Acs had at his command. And Cade was just as appalled, and tense, waiting for what he guessed would come next.

'When we first met at the Angels Bar,' Acs's empty voice went on, 'I concluded that your possession of the original slice would pose no problem for me. But, largely because of it, you have proved to be a considerable nuisance. So – I now require you to give up the slice, which I assume is hidden on your person.'

Cade took a breath for another curt reply. But he was stopped – and startled into speechlessness – when Acs continued.

'I also require you,' he said, 'to reveal where you have now hidden Fse-Yg.'

*　　*　　*

Astonishment at least kept Cade from blurting out the truth – that he had thought *Acs* had the elusive alien. And before he could think of anything at all to say, Graklin intervened.

'I'm surprised,' the old man said to Acs dryly, 'that all your expert info-searching can't turn him up.'

Acs moved his expressionless gaze towards him. 'It is less difficult to search for an inanimate object, or for info-data, than for a living and mobile being. As one called the Datamaster must know. Taking you captive is the more efficient way to acquire what I need.' He turned stiffly back to Cade. 'First, then, the data-slice.'

'Whistle for it,' Cade snapped.

Still the man's bony face showed no reaction. 'That is not wise,' he said stonily. 'I intend to acquire both the data-slice and Fse-Yg, even if I must inflict pain and mutilation to do so.'

Cade stared back into those blank frigid eyes, wishing there was something he could do or that anyone could do. But he was helpless, as they were all helpless. Their soligel bonds might resist even the power of Raishe's hype. Yet, still, Cade stubbornly told himself, there might be a chance I haven't thought of yet. Stall him, till Raishe wakes up . . .

'Being tied up has a bad effect on my memory,' he said, still holding the stare with Acs.

Acs remained still for a moment, again as if considering the statement. 'Very well,' he said tonelessly at last, gesturing to his four men, who moved forward. 'Since the woman remains unconscious, we shall begin with your great-uncle – until you co-operate.'

While two of the men stood watchfully with pyro-rifles ready, one of the others took out the glittering slimness of an ice-blade. With its scalpel-sharp edge he sliced through the bonds holding Graklin as easily as if the soligel had liquefied.

Acs stared emptily at the old man's thin, crippled legs. 'Use your rifles on his feet,' he told the other men. 'He may retain feeling in his legs, though he has no use of them.'

As the riflemen aimed their pyros, Cade saw that he had run out of time for stalling. 'Hold it,' he said quickly. 'I've got the slice under my left arm, hidden under a patch of synthoskin.'

At once Acs halted the gunmen, gesturing to the one with the knife, who stepped towards Cade.

'You want us to gel up the old cripple again?' asked another man.

Acs glanced briefly at the motionless, ashen-faced Graklin. 'No, just watch him,' he said. 'He is helpless as he is. And I may need to use him to make Cade co-operative over Fse-Yg as well.'

They all gathered around Cade then, three pointing their rifles while the knifeman cut away the soligel bonds from his upper body, leaving his legs bound. While the knifeman held his blade at Cade's throat, Acs pulled up his shirt on the left side where the syntho-skin patch could be seen, faintly, on his flesh.

A moment later, Acs had the innocuous-looking slice in his hand, his face as devoid of triumph as of any other expression.

'I will need to examine it,' he said to his men, 'to be sure it is what I seek. Wait here, and watch them.'

He turned and left the room, as swiftly and silently as he had entered it. And Cade studied the four men, weighing his chances of doing something useful while Acs was gone and his arms were free.

'You couldn't loosen this a bit, could you?' he said to the knifeman, gesturing at the soligel coils around his legs. 'It's cutting off the circulation to my feet.'

The knifeman chortled unpleasantly. 'Forget it, kid. You're stayin' as you are till Mister Acs says different.' He brought the glinting blade up to Cade's face. 'An' if you try anythin', I'll be cuttin' off more'n your circulation . . .'

Cade stared at the lethal knife, trying to find a winning smile, trying to think of something to try next. But in that desperate moment, without

164

warning, the entire room seemed to heave and shudder all around them – with the force of a huge explosion, somewhere outside, that shook the walls and blasted out the glass of every window.

15

Mayhem and Madness

One of the riflemen dashed to the nearest window, stumbling as a second massive detonation shook the building. He peered out wide-eyed.

'It's a *war* out there!' he cried.

The other men with rifles rushed forward to see for themselves. But the knifeman hung back, mindful of Acs's order to watch the prisoners, yet glancing desperately from the shattered windows to the door as if hoping for Acs to reappear and tell him what to do.

'What's goin' *on*?' he yelled at the others.

'A big fire-fight!' one of the riflemen shouted. 'There's a bunch of Phibs, looks like they got grenades as well as vipers – an' some guys in suits, shootin' at 'em – an' our boys are shootin' from the windows – an' there's Civs all over the place, shootin' at everybody . . .!'

As if to illustrate his words, a pyro-beam blasted a chunk out of the window-frame by the speaker's head, just as one of the other riflemen at another window grunted and fell straight backwards, rigid with a paralyzing Occian viper-dart. The two remaining riflemen then began firing from their windows – while the knifeman still stood indecisively near Cade, staring towards the battle.

With all those distractions, Cade took the chance to use his freed hands and all his wiry strength to tug and heave at the soligel still binding his legs, trying to push its coils downwards and slide out of their grasp. As he struggled, he cheered silently when an erratic pyro-blast from outside struck and half-melted the rifle in the hands of one of the two remaining men at the windows. But as that man fell back with a howl, the knifeman glanced away from the battle for another anxious look at the door – and saw what Cade was doing.

'You—!' he raged. Then he called to the one un-harmed rifleman. 'Come on! They're all prob'ly after these three! We gotta get 'em outa here an' find the boss!'

He reached towards Cade, ice-blade glittering. But at the window the third and last of his com-rades shrieked and collapsed, his limbs jerking with the spasms of a rattler-blast. Cursing, on his own, the knifeman gripped Cade's shirt with his free hand.

'*You're* comin', anyways,' he spat. 'I reckon you're the one the boss wants most. You give me any trouble an' I'll cripple you.'

He was holding the knife threateningly near Cade's throat as he spoke. But then, as another grenade-blast outside shook the broken window-frames, he made the mistake of looking away. And both of Cade's hands flashed up to clamp onto the wrist of his knife-hand.

The man was sinewy and strong, and fought furiously to get free. But Cade was desperate, hanging on with all his strength, and at the same time trying to twist the man's arm backwards, in the hope that the flailing blade might do some damage to its wielder. As the deadly struggle went on, Cade would have given anything to have his legs free, to be mobile. But in the end there was no need.

He had a sudden glimpse of someone coming into view behind the jerking, heaving shoulders of the knifeman. Then there was a crunching thud – and the man fell away as if he had suddenly become boneless.

And over him, holding the broken remains of a pyro-rifle with which he had clubbed the man, stood Eyr Graklin.

He was pale and sweaty and shaky, his face twisted in a grimace of anguish and determination, his spindly legs seeming about to give way under him. But he was standing.

'Grak!' Cade cried, astonished, as the old man stooped unsteadily to pick up the ice-blade. 'What . . . How can you . . .?'

'Explanations later, Jaxie,' Graklin said, cutting carefully at the soligel binding Cade's legs. 'It's painful for me to stand, so . . . you must take charge now . . .'

Abruptly he sank to the floor, groaning, as if his legs had given way. Dazedly and automatically, Cade took the knife to finish the job of freeing himself. Then he looked around, still dazedly, as if not sure what to do next, and found himself staring into Raishe's pale eyes, wide open and glaring.

'You're awake!' he said blankly.

'I've been awake all along,' she snapped. 'Get me *out* of this!'

He hurried to her, slicing carefully at the bonds that held her on the metal wheel while she warily watched the smashed windows beyond which the thunderous four-way battle was still raging.

'If we can get to the barge, can you fly it?' she asked tersely.

'I think so,' Cade said. 'Grak can help if there's anything in the guidance system I can't handle . . .'

But before he could continue, one of the window-frames was suddenly filled with the bulging-eyed form of an Occian – who paused in the narrow opening, stared at them, then levelled his viper-gun.

Cade whirled, knife in hand, knowing he could never reach the window before the alien fired.

And then he and Raishe both flinched with shock – for the scorching flame of a pyro-gun blazed down from above, from one of the skylights, towards the window where the Occian stood. And though the shot missed its target, its force flung the Occian backwards, out of view.

Then Cade and Raishe stared in amazement as a slender rope dropped from that skylight. And down the rope, with athletic ease, a shiny pyro-gun in one hand and a dazzling smile on his face, slid Hyrd Hempel.

As he bounded towards them, Raishe was smiling with delighted surprise. 'Hyrd!' she cried. 'How did you get here?'

'With the CIA team,' he said. 'They spotted a small army of Phibs heading this way and followed – after alerting the Civil Patrol . . .'

Raishe brushed the explanation aside. 'Can you help us get away?'

'Away?' Hempel repeated blankly. He gestured at the windows, at the sounds of the continuing battle outside. 'But my people . . . They want Cade, you know – and there's the Civs . . .'

Raishe's eyes blazed. 'Hyrd, he's my prisoner, and I'm getting him onto that Starliner! If you won't help me, just be sure you don't get in my way!'

'But, Raishe . . .' Hempel stared at her, looking puzzled. 'The Starliner's *gone*! It left earlier today, on schedule!'

Raishe went as white and still as an alabaster statue. Then she turned slowly to glare down at Graklin, where he still sat huddled on the floor.

'That call I made, to the spaceport . . .' she choked. 'It was a *trick*! You *rigged* it!'

The old man moved a hand feebly. 'He *is* my great-nephew . . .'

She whirled then towards Cade, as if to include him in her expanding outrage. But before she could speak, the furious storm of battle beyond that chamber finally moved inside.

A troop of Occians came lunging through the windows at the side of the room, vipers aimed.

A group of CIA men came crashing through the windows at the end of the room and fired at the Occians, who fired back.

And a surging, jostling crowd of Civil Patrolmen came bursting through the door and fired in a great many directions all at once.

As the air around and above them suddenly filled with viper darts, rattler beams and pyro blasts, Cade sprang to the wooden rack where he had been tied, heaved it over on its side, then turned to pull Graklin behind that meagre shelter. Hempel reached out to Raishe, as if to take her to join them there, but froze. Because her eyes were turning crimson.

The hype flared within her and exploded. She spun away in a blur, just as a viper dart zipped through the space where she had been standing.

Hempel stumbled back, caught himself, then ducked down behind Cade's shelter, looking dazed, while the battle raged and flamed around them.

'If you're not going to use that pyro,' Cade snapped, 'give it here.'

Hempel blinked at the gun in his hand, then held it out. 'Take it,' he croaked. 'I've got a spare.'

Wordlessly Cade took the gun while Hempel drew a second pyro from an inner pocket. Then they both peered carefully over the rack, around the room.

Where the flashing shadow that was Raishe was creating mayhem and madness.

And she had an extra weapon besides her own berserker strength and speed. She had snatched up a length of the soligel bonds that had been cut away from them, doubling it over with uncanny strength and using it as a club. At first all the scattered crowd of gunmen were too busy shooting at and dodging one another to notice her. But they began to take notice, at last, when the blur of speed and power wielding the soligel club carved a path of pain among them like a flame through dry grass.

Cade could only watch, at first, since no one was particularly shooting at him and he was afraid of hitting Raishe if he fired. She seemed to be in a great many places at once and, wherever she was, gunmen fell. Her shiny soligel weapon was as much of a blur as she was, whirling and flailing, striking and lashing. Hammer-blows flung Occians and CIA men back out of the windows, clubbed Civs to the floor, scattered groaning or unconscious bodies around the room. She picked up a Patrolman one-handed and hurled him into a cluster of his fellows who were huddled by the door. Then she scythed through the remainder of that group, flinging them aside like cut weeds, pausing for a microsecond to kick one of them accurately in the belly as he fired wildly at the place where she had just been.

But some latecomers were still rushing into the chamber, through the windows and the door, which allowed Cade and Hempel finally to join in. Neither was a crack shot, but the pyro-flame was always effective even without a direct hit. An Occian was hurled back from a window as the entire frame was incinerated around him. A pair of Civs fell, rolling and yelling, when a near-miss set their uniforms alight. And with more pyro blasts and rattler beams slicing the air around them, and occasional viper darts thudding into their wooden shield, Cade and Hempel began to seem almost in competition.

Hempel dropped an Occian with a searing shot that painfully grazed the lizard-face . . . Cade blasted a weapon out of a Civ's hand with a lucky snap shot . . . Hempel missed an Occian, but with the shot brought a chunk of plastiwall down on the alien's head . . . Cade felled a CIA man with a quick shot that scorched his shoulder . . .

'No – he's *CIA*!' Hempel protested in a burst of belated loyalty.

'If they shoot at me, they get shot at,' Cade growled, firing at a running Civ and missing.

But by then fewer people were shooting at them. Raishe was still in action, still moving like a vengeful whirlwind, sweeping through and around the conflict, leaving stunned or whimpering bodies in her wake. Until finally a moment came when Cade and Hempel both fired at the same Occian, missed, watched Raishe flash past to chop the alien down – and realized with a jolt of astonishment that he was the last.

Silence descended, save for a few muffled cries of pain outside the building. No more enemies were appearing at the windows or through the door. No one else was left standing in that chamber except Cade and Hempel behind their barrier, and Raishe – who had come to a halt, as if regaining solid form, in the absence of further opponents.

Then, to Cade's bewilderment, she flashed away again, the fury of the hype still upon her. But it had been redirected – against the vile contents of that chamber. It was as if the implements and devices of horror stirred her wrath as much as armed attack. And she stormed through the chamber like an avenging demon of demolition.

In the process, she flung the soligel aside in favour of more sturdy weapons – heavy axes, thick metal prods, long steel tongs – selected and discarded in succession as they broke or crumpled in that brutal attack. With them and the focused power of her fists and feet she reduced heavy wooden benches and platforms to kindling, pounded metal frameworks into bent and broken scrap, smashed ceramistone containers into rubble, flung deadly alien life-forms into the vat of acid. So great was her fury that she was able to hurl the bulky wheel, where she had been bound, halfway across the room, following up to smash and shatter it with a torrent of crushing blows.

Finally, after using a steel leg ripped from the wreckage of a rack to pulverize a heavy wooden pillory, she spun away to seek her next target – and halted, as if again re-materializing from the shadowy blur of her high-speed movement. Staring around with a surprised expression, she could see that there was nothing else left to destroy.

The torture chamber was entirely in ruins, its wreckage heaped and strewn among all the damaged or unconscious bodies of the gunmen. Not the smallest thumb-screw, not the lightest whip, remained intact – except for the one up-turned wooden rack that had been protecting

Cade, Graklin and Hempel.

Slowly, in a stillness that seemed as unnatural as her previous speed, Raishe turned her head towards Cade, her eyes blank and unseeing.

Then her eyes closed, and she crumpled to the floor.

Cade started to clamber over the rack to go to her, with Hempel following, but then a sudden movement at the door caught his eye and he froze, tightening his grip on the pyro-gun.

Two men stepped into view, filling the doorway. One was short and bulky, his mouth twisted in a snarl, clutching a pyro-rifle. And next to him, empty-handed and empty-eyed, stood the lean, menacing figure of Acs, surveying the wrecked chamber, then shifting his gaze to stare at Cade.

They held the stare for an instant that seemed to extend indefinitely. Then the squat rifleman whipped up his gun and fired – at exactly the same time that Cade fired, from his half-unbalanced position straddling the overturned rack.

Both were snap shots, not properly aimed, and both missed. The other man's fiery blast sizzled past Cade almost near enough to singe his hair. And Cade's own shot blazed a good hand's breadth past the rifleman's bulging midriff.

But though it missed that mark, Cade's shot hit another.

Acs staggered back, eyes suddenly wide with

shock, mouth opening in a soundless cry, the front of his tunic erupting into flames.

The bulky rifleman beside him turned, horrified. And before Cade could move, the heavy door swung shut, hiding the two of them from view.

'Let's get after them!' Hempel cried, clambering over the rack.

'Not today,' Cade said flatly. 'We're getting out of here.'

Hempel turned as if to argue – and found himself looking into the muzzle of Cade's pyro-gun.

Calmly Cade plucked the other man's gun from his hand. 'You're going to carry Raishe,' Cade told him. 'And I'm going to take Grak. Then we're going to go and find the strato-barge or something else to get us off this mountain.'

Hempel blinked. 'You won't get away, you know.'

'Won't I?' Cade gestured with his other hand. 'Look around. Listen to how quiet it's gone outside. There's no one left to stop me.' He gestured with the gun. 'And if *you* try anything, you'll find out what pyro-flame feels like. Let's go.'

And so they went – with a pause while Cade carefully and tensely opened the door a crack and peered through. Only to find that the corridor beyond it was quite empty, save for a few charred shreds of cloth on the floor.

16

A Debt to Pay

'I still think,' Raishe said coolly, 'that it was a childish and spiteful thing to do.'

Cade sighed. She was talking about what had happened after he and Hempel had carried Raishe and Graklin on to the strato-barge. The barge had been where they had left it, quite unharmed, and they had no trouble reaching it. There had been a great many sprawled and groaning bodies around the complex of buildings – Phibs and Civs, CIA agents and Acs's thugs – but none of them had been mobile or interested enough to do anything about the four survivors.

Inside the barge, after Hempel had placed Raishe's limp form on a sofa and Cade had helped Graklin into a chair, Cade had calmly stuck the pyro-gun under the blond man's nose and backed him up – all the way off the barge. He then closed its hatch in his face and took off.

'It was the smart thing to do,' Cade said wearily, going to pour a drink from the lounge's ample supply. 'The CIA's after me as much as anyone.'

She sniffed. 'You did it because you don't like him. Even though he came to our rescue, in a way.'

'That doesn't win him any prizes,' Cade growled. 'Why do you care, anyway? Did you have plans for him?' He grinned at her glare. 'Never mind – you might run into him again, since we missed the Starliner.'

Tight-lipped, she rose smoothly to her feet, turned her back on Cade and stalked over to a window-port. Beyond it the Tallyran dawn was painting a rosiness on the clouds below the strato-barge, which was cruising on auto-guide. The two of them were on their own, since Graklin had gone to rest. But before that he had settled himself in a spare servo-chair that he kept on the barge – and had explained about the ailment that caused pain and weakness in the bones of his legs, but that did *not* leave him as wholly disabled as he had always seemed.

'I never wanted to deceive you, Jaxie,' the old man had said before he had left them alone. 'But it has been useful to appear more helpless than I am, to potential enemies.' He had smiled apologetically. 'Certainly it proved a useful deception tonight . . .'

At the window-port, Raishe wheeled away from the view of the dawn to aim her glare at Cade again. 'In fact, we didn't *miss* the Starliner, as you put it. Your sneaky great-uncle performed another of his *deceptions*. You're *both* a pair of spiteful, lying tricksters.'

'Thanks very much,' Cade replied calmly. 'And now, since we aren't on our way back to Breell, I think it's time you took this collar off me.'

As he spoke, he rested a hand meaningfully on the pyro-gun tucked in his belt. But Raishe merely glanced at it, with a delicate snort.

'Or else you'll shoot me, is that it?' she said through her teeth. And then she moved – not at the eerie, blurred speed of the hype, yet swiftly enough to snatch the gun from his belt before he could react. 'No,' she went on, hefting the gun in her hand, 'the collar stays.'

Cade looked pained. 'Come on, Raishe. It's getting so I can't breathe with it on.'

She snorted again. 'I suppose you want to be free to go chasing around the Sewer again, looking for that Fse *and* trying to get the slice back from Acs.'

'That's only half right,' he told her. 'I don't need to get the slice back, because Acs hasn't got it.' He patted his side, under his right arm. 'I bought a blank slice at that maxi-store, and hid it in the syntho-skin under my left arm. The real one's on *this* side, even better hidden.'

She stared at him disbelievingly. 'But he went to *check* the slice, after he took it off you . . .! He might have *crippled* you when he found it was a fake!'

Cade shrugged. 'I was trying to buy some time . . . Anyway, it worked, didn't it? We got away. Why get heated up about something that didn't happen?'

'One day,' she said icily, 'that unnatural luck of yours is going to run out. And a whole *lifetime* of disaster is going to come crashing down on you.'

'Probably,' he agreed, grinning. 'So I might as well have some fun, and make some money, before then.' He lifted his drink in a mock-toast. 'And I *do* still want to look for Fse-Yg, since we're still here.'

'I wouldn't bother, Jax,' said Graklin's voice from the doorway. 'If you look for Fse-Yg on Tallyra, you'll be looking in the wrong place.'

'I thought you were resting,' Cade said, startled. 'And what do you mean, about the Fse?'

Looking troubled, Graklin floated his chair into the room. 'I couldn't rest – not with so many loose ends bothering me. So I set up some new info-searches – looking for Acs, at first.'

'And . . .?' Cade prompted.

The old man sighed wearily. 'Nothing. Not the smallest trace of him, anywhere. Alive or dead, he's being kept well hidden.'

'I wouldn't think he's too healthy after taking

that pyro-blast,' Cade said unconcernedly. 'What about Fse-Yg?'

'I tapped into the spaceport data-banks,' Graklin said, 'wondering if Acs might have left Tallyra. But instead, I found that it's Fse-Yg who has gone off-planet. On the Starliner . . .' He glanced apologetically towards Raishe, who glared. 'Obviously, he won enough at that gambling club to afford the fare.'

Cade sank into a chair, looking stricken. 'Where's he heading?'

'To a remote planet,' Graklin said with a pleased smile, 'where, as I discovered earlier, he once lived. Lannamur.'

'The world with the high-tech moons!' Cade said.

'Exactly,' Graklin confirmed. 'And there's more. One of my continuing auto-searches, which has gone on running, has discovered – among fragments of records that have been altered or partly erased – that Fse-Yg once worked on the moons of Lannamur. As an info-tech worker . . .'

'Just stop it there,' Raishe broke in. 'Next you'll be saying you've located an operational Artificial Intelligence on this Lannamur.'

'No,' Graklin admitted. 'I've still found no trace at all of any surviving AI. But the other connections are interesting.'

'More than that,' Cade said excitedly. 'Especially with Acs out of the picture . . .'

'I said stop it,' Raishe snapped. 'I don't care about Acs or the slice or where Fse-Yg is going. It's all *over*. From now on, Cade, the only important thing is where *you're* going.' She gestured with the gun. 'I want you to take the barge down now. Then we'll find a place to stay – where I *will* keep you shackled till the next Starliner docks. As I should have done in the first place.'

Graklin cleared his throat. 'In fact, Raishe . . . there isn't a great deal of point in that.'

'Why not?' she demanded.

'First,' the old man said mildly, 'even if you were to do as you say, and even though Acs does seem to be out of things, the Occians and the CIA are still in the hunt. Perhaps feeling *vengeful*, after what happened on the mountain.'

Raishe's mouth tightened. 'Is that supposed to frighten me? We can stay safely hidden as long as we need to.'

'I've got a great idea for a hiding-place,' Cade said brightly. 'If we could get off Tallyra . . .'

'No, you don't!' Raishe cried. 'We're going to do as I said – dig in somewhere here and wait for the Starliner!'

Graklin smiled gently at her. 'There's something else that you should know, Raishe, before you make too many plans.'

'Such as?' she asked.

'Shortly after you and Jaxie first arrived,' the old man said, almost apologetically, 'I began to set up another process. Actually a *series* of processes.'

'What have you done?' Raishe demanded tensely.

Graklin made a vague gesture. 'On Tallyra, I've spread a little cash around – so the Civil Patrol will no longer concern themselves with Jaxie. But before that, more importantly, I set up a special *trespass* procedure over the interstellar links, and slipped into the data-field of the planet Breell. Shielded all the way, of course, so as not to be detected. And, once in, the trespass made . . . adjustments to certain data-stores. Those memories now contain reports that an escaped prisoner named Jaxie Cade met his *death*, accidentally, on a world in the Pilifar system. So his files have been labelled "inactive". And I fear that your contract to retrieve him, Raishe, has been cancelled.'

'Uncle Grak!' Cade said fervently, eyes wide with joy.

But Raishe's expression had been slowly changing while Graklin was speaking, her face growing taut and flushed, her pale eyes ablaze. And her arm came up to level the pyro-gun at the old man's face.

'You . . .' She was almost unable to speak in her rage. 'You slippery, slimy, sneaky, spiteful old . . . *crook*!'

'Oh, indeed,' Graklin murmured. 'Undeniably.'

Cade laughed boisterously. 'If you shoot us both, Raishe, you'll have to land the barge by yourself.'

She ignored him, still glaring at Graklin. 'Does your terminal here have an interstellar facility?'

Graklin looked mildly puzzled. 'Of course . . .'

'And is it rigged with any more of your evil little tricks?'

'Not at all,' Graklin said, frowning. 'Why do you ask?'

She swung the gun from one to the other. 'Because I'm going to make a call. And you two can stay quiet, here, and no games.'

As she whirled away to the adjoining room that held the Netlink, Cade turned anxiously to Graklin. 'Won't she be able to reverse what you did,' he asked, 'if she proves I'm alive?'

'I doubt it,' the old man said, almost sadly. 'Regrettably, I had to arrange for her to . . . lose some credibility.'

In a surprisingly short time, Raishe returned. And where before she had been flushed with anger, the towering fury that filled her then had turned her face stark white and her eyes incandescent. It was almost as if she was on the edge of the hype, and both men quailed slightly as she confronted them.

'I ought to use this!' she choked, aiming the gun at Graklin. 'I ought to make you the total cripple you pretend to be!'

'Raishe . . .' Cade said nervously. 'What happened?'

'I've lost my *job*!' she rasped. 'Someone seems to have told the PReD high command that I *faked* a search for a fugitive – a *dead* one – so I could have a free holiday on Tallyra! And they've fired me!'

Cade smiled weakly. 'You weren't happy in the job anyway . . .'

She swung towards him, making him flinch. 'Maybe not – but it was *my* choice if I left, and when! Not yours or Graklin's or anyone's!' She whirled back to face Graklin again. 'You've just wrecked my life, you scheming old snake! I'll be *unemployable* now, with that on my record . . .!'

Graklin sighed. 'I know, and I do regret it. But you must see, I couldn't let anything happen to Jaxie.'

'So you made it happen to me!' Raishe spat. 'But now it's the other way around, old man. You're going to pay. You've robbed me and ruined me, so you *owe* me – and you're going to *pay*!'

Graklin drew back slightly. 'I doubt whether it's entirely legal, even on Tallyra, to demand money at gun-point.'

For a still and soundless moment Raishe held her stance, her hand growing white-knuckled on the gun's grip. At last, slowly, that hand drooped, while her face twisted into a mask of frustration and despair as well as fury. Silently she turned and stalked away to stare blankly out of a window-port again, trembling as she fought to keep control.

Behind her, as Graklin sagged in his chair with relief, Cade had begun to look thoughtful.

'You know, Grak,' he said, pitching his voice so that she could hear, 'Raishe is right. We have messed up her life – and we do owe her something.'

'Of course,' Graklin said at once. 'I'm quite happy to help her – perhaps with the fare for the next Starliner . . .'

'I was thinking of another sort of help, for Raishe and me both,' Cade said intently. 'Do you know any way for us to get off the Edge, quickly, right now?'

'I imagine so,' Graklin said with a puzzled frown, 'if you wish. I know someone with a freighter who makes regular runs off-planet. But it has no real provision for passengers . . .'

'Doesn't matter,' Cade said. 'If you could get us on it – and maybe manage a loan . . .'

That brought Raishe around to scowl at them, suspicion joining the anger and misery in her expression. 'What game are you playing now?'

'No game,' Cade assured her. 'An *idea* . . . For a way that you *could* be repaid for what you've lost . . . and then some.' He offered his most sincere smile. 'I think we should continue our partnership. With Grak's help, we can head for this planet, Lannamur, without delay – to find Fse-Yg and get the rest of the info on the Phantom Planet!'

'You're *insane*,' she breathed.

'Maybe,' Cade agreed, 'but just think about it. We don't have much to lose, now, either of us, and we'd have a whole *world* to gain.' His smile became a cajoling grin. 'And we make a great team . . .'

'I'd certainly be glad to help,' Graklin added.

They watched her carefully, then, as she stared silently back at them, still looking suspicious and furious and distressed all at once. But as the silence went on, Cade felt certain that he could see the return of the giveaway gleam in her eyes, the gleam of interest and temptation and something almost like hunger.

'You really do have the most incredible nerve,' she said to Cade at last, her voice taut. 'A *team* . . .?'

Cade shrugged, smiling. 'We've done pretty well so far.'

'And the Phantom Planet,' Graklin put in, 'would be a prize almost beyond measure – even divided three ways.'

She shook her head slowly, but the gleam was even more evident in her eyes. 'I can't believe this is happening . . . But you can stop selling the idea. I'm well aware that if we *did* get the info on the Phantom Planet, it would be worth a fortune – whether the Planet really exists or not.'

'Then you agree?' Cade said eagerly.

'Not entirely,' Raishe told him, her eyes flashing. 'You can forget all about being a team or partnership or whatever. Instead of being your partner, I'm going to be your *creditor*.'

Cade looked taken aback, but Graklin nodded. 'Even so, you'd still need to go with Jaxie to Lannamur. To protect your investment.'

'Oh, yes,' Raishe said acidly. 'I should think it'll need protecting, with you two playing your crooked games.'

Cade's grin was knowing. 'But that's not the only reason, is it, Raishe? You'll be going because you're as deeply hooked as I am by the Phantom Planet, the whole mystery and dream of it . . .'

She shrugged. 'All you need to think about, Cade, is that I'm going with you to make sure I get what's owed to me.'

'If you say so,' he replied, still grinning. 'But since you *are* going, and since we *will* be working together, how about taking this collar off me?'

She fixed him with her most withering glare. 'You don't listen, do you?' she said coldly. 'Try to understand, Cade, so there won't be any mistakes. We may be travelling together for a while, to Lannamur or wherever – but we won't be *partners*, and the collar stays. Until I get compensation for what's been done to me.' She glanced at Graklin to include him in her glare. 'Also, if we do manage to get any more info on the Phantom Planet, we're going to *sell* it – a legitimate, *honest* sale. And I'm going to want at least *half* the proceeds, because of all the trouble you've caused me. And because you're such a complete pain in the backside!'

Cade's grin had gone a little lopsided as he fingered the restraint collar at his throat. 'We can talk about all that again, another time,' he said quickly. 'For now, I'll promise you one thing – if we have any luck at all, you'll be the richest ex-PReD in the galaxy.' He turned to Graklin. 'Now, what about this freighter, Grak? How near does it go to Lannamur?'

THE END